Capta
and The ice Queen

Sheila K. McCullagh

ARNOLD-WHEATON
A Division of Pergamon Press

The Towers of the Snow People

Hornwollen's Island

T
B

The M
Home
Snow F

Sheep Pastures

The Home of the North

The Wide River

The Country of the People of the Snow

h
elds

e South
Berry Fields

in
e

N

W E

S

Seal Island

When Nicholas's great-uncle Jeremy was lost at sea, he left Nicholas a picture. It was a picture of a great ring of silver, against a black background. There was a picture inside the silver ring, too. Most of the time, it was just the sea and the sky. But sometimes the picture changed and Nicholas found himself looking right through the ring, into another country.

In some strange way, when the ring glowed like silver fire it grew very large, and Nicholas found himself moving right through it, into the country in the centre of the ring.

Sometimes, he found himself on a ship; sometimes on dry land. But wherever he was, he found himself among the buccaneers of Ramir, who had become his friends.

This is another of Nicholas's adventures.

Chapter 1
Orders from Ramir

Nicholas had had a long day at school. They had been learning about sailing ships, in the days before steamships had been invented. If anyone talked about sailing ships, Nicholas always thought about the buccaneers of Ramir, and *The Silver Dolphin*. His teacher had been surprised at how much Nicholas knew about sailing. Nicholas went to bed, still thinking about Ramir.

As soon as he shut his eyes, pictures began to form against his eyelids. He felt as if he were a bird, flying high over the sea. Far below him, he saw the city of Ramir, hidden among the mountains. He saw the long Sea Road between the mountains, leading to the gates of the city. As he watched, the gates opened, and he saw a wide square, with a fountain playing in the middle. Beyond the fountain, there was a great stone building, filling one side of the square.

The picture faded. Nicholas opened his eyes and sat up in bed. The room was dark. He looked across at the wall, where the picture of the silver ring hung in the darkness. But there was no light coming from the ring. He could scarcely see it, against the dark wall.

He sighed deeply. Every bit of him was beginning to feel excited, just as he always felt when he was going back to Ramir. And yet the silver ring looked as dull as if it had been cut out of cardboard.

And then, just as he was going to lie down again, the ring began to glow.

At first he wasn't sure. He wanted it to shine so much, that he thought he must be imagining it. But as he watched, the glow grew brighter. The ring seemed to stand out from the picture, almost as if it was hanging in the middle of the room.

Nicholas threw back the bedclothes, and sprang out of bed. He crossed over to the ring, and stood there waiting. He was much too excited to stand still, and he hopped first on one foot and then on the other.

The ring grew brighter and brighter. Slowly, a picture began to form in the middle of it.

He saw a little, dark room, not much bigger than a cupboard. Light was shining into the room through a carving on one of the walls.

Nicholas drew in his breath. He remembered that room. He had been there before. It was a secret room, hidden in the wall of the great building in the square. The Council of Ramir met in the big room on the other side of that carved screen.

The silver light in the ring blazed out. Nicholas stepped quickly into it. For a moment, it flared all around him. Then it died away, and he found himself standing once more in the secret room.

He stepped quickly to the carving, and looked through into the room beyond.

The room was lit by lanterns, hanging from brackets in the walls, and a fire was blazing under a great stone chimney at one end.

Twenty men and three women were sitting around the long table in the middle of the room. Nicholas knew some of them. Captain Harken was sitting on the far side of the table, and Captain James, the High Captain of Ramir, was sitting at one end.

At the other end of the table, there was a dark-haired man with fierce eyes, and a nose like a bird's beak. He was dressed in a jacket of white and silver and he had a grey cloak, trimmed with white fur. Nicholas saw a ring on his finger. A ruby, which was set in the golden ring, flashed like red fire.

A boy, who was not much older than Nicholas, sat by the man's side. Nicholas didn't know the man, but he knew the boy. It was the Alarkin, the younger son of the Lord of Ramir. The Alarkin looked pale and thin, as if he had been ill.

The dark-haired man was speaking.

"The question is decided," he said. "Captain James will sail north in *The Ice Queen*. He will bring back as many sacks of snow-berries as he can, and he will arrange for more sacks of snow-berries to be sent to Ramir every year from the far north.

"Captain Harken has sailed to the north

before. He knows the Arcons, and he knows the People of the Snow. He will sail north with Captain James.''

''I am still against the whole idea, Soluken,'' said Captain Harken quietly. ''We have enough snow-berries for all our needs for a long time. These were given to us by the People of the Snow. They asked only one thing in return: they asked to be left in peace.

''The snow-berries cured our people when they were ill. If the great sickness had come back to Ramir, we should have a reason for going north. But the sickness has passed. The people of Ramir are well. We should leave the People of the Snow in peace.''

''I think Captain Harken is right, Soluken,'' said the Alarkin quietly.

Soluken's face grew red and his eyes flashed.

''We have talked this over for three hours,'' he said. Nicholas could hear the anger in his voice. ''Let me remind you, Alarkin, that I am the Regent of Ramir, until you are old enough to be king. You are too young to decide these matters.

''As for you, Captain Harken, you have already told us what you think. The Council of Ramir has decided against you. Unfortunately, you are the only captain who has sailed in the far north before.

''You will sail there in *The Snow Goose,* and you will sail under Captain James' orders. Is that understood?''

8

"Very well," said Captain Harken quietly.

"Captain James couldn't have a better man with him, when he is going to sail into the dangerous seas of the north," said one of the Council.

"No one questions Captain Harken's seamanship," said Soluken. "We know that he has sailed ships from Ramir to the ends of the earth."

He turned to Captain Harken.

"All you have to do, Captain Harken," he said, "is to obey orders, and sail your ship."

Captain Harken looked at Soluken, and then at Captain James, who was sitting opposite to him. But he said nothing.

Soluken looked at the people sitting around the table.

"Are there any more questions?" he asked. "No? Then we will end this meeting of the Council. Captain James, I should like a few words with you."

He pushed back his chair, and got up. Everyone else got to their feet. Soluken and Captain James went out of a little door on Nicholas's right, at one end of the room. The others moved to a big door which led into the passage.

Nicholas turned quickly to the wooden panel in the opposite wall of the little room. He slid the panel sideways, and slipped through the hole into the passage beyond.

He had just time to slide the wooden panel

back into place, before the Alarkin and Captain Harken came out into the passage.

"Nicholas!" cried Captain Harken, stepping forward and holding out his hand. "Nicholas! How long have you been here?"

"I've only just come," said Nicholas.

"I'm glad to see you," said the Alarkin. "You'll be sailing with Captain Harken! I wish I was! But they won't let me go."

"The Alarkin is King of Ramir now, Nicholas," said Captain Harken.

"Not really king, until I'm crowned," said the Alarkin. "I don't know when that will be. They say I'm too young. Until I'm crowned, Soluken is Regent. He rules Ramir."

"You remember that the Lord of Ramir died in the great sickness, Nicholas," said Captain Harken quietly.

"Yes," said Nicholas. "I remember."

"The snow-berries came too late for my father," said the Alarkin, "but they came in time to save me. I was very ill when *The Snow Goose* sailed into the Sea Road of Ramir, with the sacks of snow-berries. They came only just in time. That was a year ago, and even now I am only just getting my strength back again.

"But we mustn't think about the past. We must think about the future. I know you don't want to go back to the north, Captain Harken. I wish no one was going, and if I were King of Ramir, the north would be left in peace.

"But if Captain James is going, I think you should go with him. If he is on his own, Captain James will deal much too harshly with the people of the north. He will expect them to obey him and he'll try to punish them if they don't. If you are there, you may be able to make friends with them."

"I think I'm friends with them now," said Captain Harken. "But I don't know whether I can keep their friendship, if we sail north again, to take still more snow-berries from them. They gave us all they could spare. Another year has passed, and there will be more berries growing on the slopes, but they will need those for themselves. I gave them my word that we would leave them in peace."

"Well, you can at least protect the People of the Snow, if you have to," said the Alarkin. "Surely Captain James will listen to you, even if Soluken won't."

Captain Harken shook his head.

"I hope so," he said, "but I doubt it."

While they were talking, they had been walking along the wide stone passage. They went down the big stone staircase at the end of the passage, and through a large hall, to two great doors.

"I will say goodbye here," said the Alarkin. "You sail first thing in the morning. Soluken won't let me go with you, so I can only wish you good luck. Remember, whatever happens, you have a friend here in

Ramir. When I am king, there will be someone here who listens to what you have to say.''

''I shall remember,'' said Captain Harken. ''Goodbye, Alarkin, King of Ramir, and thank you. I may need friends, before this is over.''

''Goodbye, Nicholas,'' said the Alarkin. ''I'm glad you're going with *The Snow Goose.* I only wish I was going with you.''

''So do I,'' said Nicholas.

The Alarkin went back across the hall, and Nicholas went out with Captain Harken into the square.

''It's a bad business, Nicholas,'' said Captain Harken, as they walked across the square and down the street that led to the gate of the city. ''For some reason, Soluken wants to get his hands on more snow-berries. I don't know why, but I think I can guess. The Alunka, who live in a country south of Ramir, would give ten sacks of gold for one of snow-berries. We could spare them some of the sacks we already have, if there was illness in Alunka. But there isn't.

''People think that the snow-berries are some kind of magic, and so they are willing to pay for them in gold, whether they need them or not.

''I don't like it, Nicholas. There are some people who would do almost anything to get hold of snow-berries. I'm afraid Soluken is one of them, and Captain James will obey his orders.

"There's one thing about it. None of us know where the People of the Snow live, so Captain James can't attack them."

Captain Harken stopped suddenly, and looked at Nicholas.

"Nicholas!" he exclaimed. "Hornwollen took you to the snow people. Did he take you to their home?"

Nicholas nodded. "Yes," he said. "But I promised them that I would never tell anyone where that was. I promised that I wouldn't tell even you."

"I'm glad of that!" said Captain Harken. "I know you well enough to be sure that you'll keep that promise. You must keep it, Nicholas. I'm not sure what Captain James will do, if the People of the Snow won't give him the berries."

He walked on slowly again, with Nicholas beside him.

"Well," he said thoughtfully, "we're under orders to go, and we have to obey orders. But I shall do my best to protect the Arcons, and the People of the Snow. Perhaps the Alarkin's right. If Captain James is going, I should go too. Captain James could find his way there without me. He's read the log of *The Snow Goose*. I wrote everything down in the log, just as it happened. The worst thing would be for Captain James to sail *The Ice Queen* there alone, with only his own men.''

''Soluken is the Regent of Ramir, isn't he?'' asked Nicholas.

''Yes, he's the Regent — the Ruler of Ramir, for the time being,'' said Captain Harken. ''When the Lord of Ramir died, the Alarkin was very ill. The Lord of Ramir had chosen the Alarkin to be ruler after him. The Alarkin had brought back the Crown of Ramir, and the people wanted to crown him king. But he's very young, and everyone thought he was going to die.

''So the Council made Soluken regent for three years. Soluken is a great friend of Captain James — or so it seems. And while he is the Regent of Ramir, Captain James will obey him.''

Captain Harken straightened himself, as if he were tossing off a burden. ''Well, that's enough of that, boy,'' he said. ''We're sailing north, and I must say I'm glad that you've come to join us. I'm always glad to see you, Nick. You know that.''

''I'm glad to be here,'' said Nicholas. ''Who's coming with us?''

''All your friends,'' said Captain Harken with a laugh. ''Barnabas, Tom Gold, Halek, Peran, Cass, Alwar — you'll know them all. Downalong Joe is boatswain now, and he's as gloomy as ever!''

Nicholas laughed. He knew that Captain Harken was worried about the voyage, but he couldn't help feeling happy that he was going to be sailing again with the buccaneers on *The Snow Goose.*

They went through the city gate, and Nicholas saw *The Snow Goose* lying at anchor, lifting and falling gently on the sea, under the stars.

Chapter 2
The voyage north

There was a great welcome for Nicholas on
The Snow Goose. Barnabas Brandy thumped
him on the back, and told him that he had
been expecting him. Tom Gold said that he
was sure, now, that they'd all get home
safely. And Halek went below, and came
back with a big bundle.

When Nicholas opened the bundle in the
great cabin, he found the warm clothes he
had worn last time in the north. They were all
washed and ready for him to put on. The
white trousers, boots and parka which the
People of the Snow had given him were there,
too, and so was the horn.

"You'll be warm, even if the rest of us
freeze to death!" said Halek cheerfully, as
Nicholas put the clothes away on the shelf in
Barnabas' cabin. "The rest of us haven't got
clothes as warm as the ones the snow people
gave you."

"I'll lend you the parka," said Nicholas.

Halek laughed. "It's too small for me," he
said. "You can keep it. You're quite safe!
Anyway, we have got ice clothes — the ones
we wore in the far south."

"Now that the donkey has arrived, Halek,
you'd better get the donkey's breakfast!" said
Barnabas Brandy, coming into the cabin.

"I've got it all ready," said Halek.

He went off, and came back with a sack of straw, to make a bed for Nicholas.

Halek dropped the sack on the floor, and Barnabas gave Nicholas two thick blankets and a pillow to make up the bed.

Nicholas knew that he wouldn't need the blankets yet. It was summer, and it was warm in Ramir. But even in summer, it is warmer on land than it is on the sea. And he would be glad of the thick blankets and the warm clothes, as they sailed north.

Nicholas took his things into the little port cabin, where Barnabas Brandy slept. As soon as he had made up his bed, he went on deck.

It was a busy scene on the quay. Captain James' ship, *The Ice Queen* was anchored beyond *The Snow Goose,* and the last stores of food and water were being loaded on to both ships. Nicholas saw great barrels of water and sacks of flour being carried aboard, and stowed away down in the hold.

A flock of goats came along the quay, driven by a boy not much older than Nicholas. The goats were driven up the gangway, bleating loudly, and hoisted down below.

The sun set, but the work still went on. The quay was lit by flaring torches. Carts, pulled by horses, moved in and out of the city gate.

A man came with a string of donkeys. Each donkey carried a great basket on either side. The baskets were full of big jars of honey, and casks of wine.

At last, everything was loaded on board. The buccaneers said goodbye to their wives and children, who had come down to see the ships sail, and the two ships left the quay. The men lined the side, waving to their families, as the ships moved out into the Sea Road, and anchored for the night.

Nicholas stood on deck, watching, as the sails were furled, and the ships anchored close to the high cliffs of the Sea Road of Ramir.

The moon rose, and shone down over the sea. *The Ice Queen* was a bigger ship than *The Snow Goose,* and she looked very beautiful in the moonlight. Nicholas could see the carved figure under her bows. It was of a woman wearing a crown. Her long hair streamed out behind her, and her hands were at her sides. She was painted silver, like the figurehead on *The Silver Dolphin.* The windows of the great cabin under the poop deck shone yellow in the darkness.

"Isn't she a beauty?" said Halek, coming over to Nicholas, and looking across at *The Ice Queen.*

"She looks bigger than *The Snow Goose,*" said Nicholas.

"So she is," said Halek. "She can sail faster, too. Captain James wouldn't have her strengthened for sailing in the ice. He said it wasn't necessary. So she isn't as heavy as *The Snow Goose.* When we're on the open sea, *The Ice Queen* will be able to out-sail us, with no trouble at all. But I'd rather be on *The Snow Goose,* if we get into an ice field.''

Nicholas slept well that night on the straw sack in the cabin. The ship lifted and fell gently under him. Barnabas Brandy, in the bunk on the other side of the cabin, snored steadily in his sleep. But Nicholas didn't hear him, even in his dreams.

* * *

The next two weeks were some of the happiest Nicholas had ever known. During the day, he was up on deck, watching the men working the ship. He ran messages for Captain Harken, and carried mugs of soup up to him when he was too busy to come to the great cabin for meals. He kept the cabin brushed out, and gave Halek a hand whenever he could.

But he still had time to watch *The Ice Queen,* gliding over the blue sea beside them in the sunlight, with her sails set and the figurehead under her bows shining in the sun.

He watched the waves, breaking white below him, as *The Snow Goose* cut through the water. He watched the seabirds flying past in the blue sky.

There were cheerful meals round the table in the great cabin. He knew that Captain Harken was worried about the voyage, but Captain Harken didn't show his feelings to the buccaneers. He took time, too, to show

Nicholas his maps and charts, and teach him more about sailing a ship. Halek taught him the names of the ropes, and Barnabas talked to him about winds and currents. He had never had a chance to learn so much before.

As they sailed farther north, it grew colder and colder. The days grew longer, and the nights grew shorter, and Nicholas knew that it was summer in the far land to the north.

One night, after a day which had seemed much colder than usual, Nicholas was standing at the ship's side, looking north. The sky was bright with stars, and as he looked, it seemed to grow brighter still.

A patch of light showed in the sky, like a silver mist. It grew brighter and brighter, until it looked like a hanging curtain of white ice. A shaft of green light stretched up from the horizon.

"It's magic! Magic!" said a voice in Nicholas's ear.

He turned, and saw Alwar by his side.

"It's the People of the Snow," whispered Alwar, almost as if he were speaking to himself. "They're lighting their magic fires in the sky!"

The lights in the sky changed and grew, until it looked as if *The Snow Goose* was sailing north under a great tent of white fire.

"It's not the People of the Snow, Alwar," said Nicholas. "It's the northern lights. It's not magic. People often see the northern lights in the sky, when they travel in the north.''

''How do you know?'' asked Alwar hoarsely. ''Only Hornwollen has travelled in the north — Hornwollen, and *The Snow Goose*. No one goes there, because of the ice. It's magic, I tell you!'' He turned and stared at Nicholas. ''What do *you* know about it?'' he demanded. ''Are you really one of the snow people yourself? Is *that* where you come from? The snow people looked after you, last time we were in the north.''

''No,'' said Nicholas. ''No. Don't think that, Alwar. There's nothing magic about me. I — I just live somewhere else.''

''But how do you get here?'' asked Alwar. Nicholas could hear the fear in his voice. ''Where do you come from? You come and go like a ghost!''

''I'm no ghost,'' said Nicholas. ''When I'm in Ramir, I'm the ship's boy on *The Snow Goose* — or *The Silver Dolphin*. There's nothing magic about me.''

''I don't believe it,'' said Alwar in a whisper. ''You're one of them. You're one of the People of the Snow!''

His eyes looked very big and dark in his white face, and Nicholas saw that he was shivering.

''I'm not one of the snow people, Alwar,'' he said. ''And I'm not a ghost. I'm just a boy.''

Alwar stood staring at him, biting his lip. Then he suddenly turned on his heel, ran across the deck, and disappeared down the hatch.

Nicholas looked after him, wondering what he could say to help him. But he thought that he had better not follow him. It would only make him more frightened.

He turned back to the sea, and gazed up into the sky at the splendour of the northern lights.

* * *

Nicholas was on deck again the next morning, when Cass, who was up in the barrel at the cross-trees, shouted: ''Land ho! Land on the port bow!''

Nicholas stared out over the water, but he couldn't see the land from the deck. He looked back, to where Captain Harken was standing on the poop deck. Halek was just running up with Captain Harken's telescope.

Captain Harken took the telescope, and looked across the sea, the way Cass was pointing.

Nicholas saw a man on *The Ice Queen* signalling to them with flags. *The Ice Queen* turned slowly west, towards the distant land, and *The Snow Goose* followed her.

Nicholas ran up on to the poop deck, to join Captain Harken and Barnabas Brandy, and to get a better look. Before long, he saw the dark line of far off hills.

"Is that the land of the Arcons?" he asked Barnabas.

"I think we're still a bit south of the bay where the Arcons live," said Barnabas. "But it may be the same country. What do you think, Francis?"

"I think it is," said Captain Harken. "Anyway, Captain James seems to want us to run in and take a look."

As they sailed nearer, they saw that they were coming into the mouth of a great river. There were green hills on each side of it, covered with little fir trees.

Captain James took *The Ice Queen* slowly in nearer the shore. *The Snow Goose* followed her. Peran was at the bows, swinging a thin line with lead on the end of it into the water. A bit of coloured cloth was tied on the line every two metres, and he called out the depth of the water as they sailed slowly in.

The Ice Queen dropped anchor when they were still some way out, and *The Snow Goose* anchored beside her.

"There's a boat coming over," said Barnabas Brandy.

Nicholas saw a boat lowered from *The Ice Queen*. Six buccaneers climbed into it, and took the oars, and then another man followed them. It was Captain James.

A few minutes later, Captain James climbed aboard *The Snow Goose*. His men stayed in the boat.

Captain Harken was on deck to greet him.

"Well, Captain Harken," said Captain James. "It's been a good voyage. I take it that this must be the land where you found one of the ships of the North Arcons?"

"We were farther north when we met them," said Captain Harken. "But I think it must be the same country. There's no map of this part of the world."

Captain James nodded. "I want to make some changes, at this point in our voyage," he said. "We will discuss them."

He walked across the deck to the door of the great cabin, opened it, and went in. Captain Harken followed him.

"I wonder what all that's about," said Tom Gold, as the door of the cabin shut behind them.

"We'll soon know," said Barnabas Brandy. "Captain James may say he wants to discuss something, but what he really means is that he's going to give some orders. It won't take long."

Barnabas Brandy was right. A few minutes later, Captain James came out on deck. Captain Harken, who was looking very worried, came with him.

Captain James glanced at Barnabas Brandy. He nodded to him, and then walked across the deck and climbed down into the boat, without saying a word to anyone.

The six men rowed the boat back to *The Ice Queen*. Captain Harken stood watching it for a minute or two. Then he turned to Barnabas Brandy.

"Come into the great cabin, Barnabas," he said. "You too, Tom. Send someone below for Downalong Joe. We'll need him as well. You come too, Nicholas."

They all followed Captain Harken into the great cabin. Captain Harken sat down at the head of the table, and the others sat down around it.

Captain Harken waited until Downalong Joe joined them. Then he looked at the faces around the table.

"Well," he said. "We've new orders from Captain James. From now on, I am to sail with him on *The Ice Queen,* to act as pilot. That's fair enough, I suppose, since I have been here before.

"I'm less happy about the other orders. Barnabas, you and Tom are to go to *The Ice Queen* with me, and so is young Nicholas.

"Captain James is going to send three of his own men to *The Snow Goose,* to take our places: Cazzek, who is first mate on *The Ice Queen,* will take over here as captain, and he will have the second and third mates from *The Ice Queen,* Fryock and Garl, to help him."

There were gasps of surprise from the men around the table.

"But why on earth would Captain James do that?" cried Barnabas Brandy. "I can see that he might take you as a pilot. You could lead the way as captain of *The Snow Goose* just as well, but Captain James isn't the man to follow another ship. His own ship always has to be first. But why does he want Tom and me? And young Nicholas, too! Why on earth should he want him?''

''I don't know, Barnabas, but I'm not happy about it,'' said Captain Harken. ''That's why I asked you to join us here, Downalong. You're the boatswain, and the men trust you. So do I. Captain Cazzek will be in charge, and Fryock and Garl will be mates on the ship.

''It may be all right. But I know Cazzek. He'll do anything Captain James tells him to. And Captain James, in his turn, will carry out Soluken's orders, whatever they may be. I think that Soluken has given him some orders which we don't know about.

''We made friends with the Arcons, when we were here in the north last year. We've eaten fish and salt with them. As you know, that's the way the Arcons make a treaty of friendship.

''We mustn't break that treaty. We've pledged our word to the Arcons, and we must keep our word, for the honour of Ramir. For ourselves, too. The Arcons will never trust us again, if we break our promise of friendship. What's more, other people will hear of it, and no one who sails the sea will ever trust us. I wouldn't trust us, myself, if we broke our word to the Arcons!

''Everything may be all right. I hope it is.

Of course you will obey Captain Cazzek's orders, Downalong — unless he orders you to break that treaty. If he does that, let me know at once. You must get a message to me, or to Tom Gold or Barnabas, any way you can.''

''Aye, aye, Cap'n!'' said Downalong Joe. ''I've sailed with Captain Cazzek myself once. I'll keep an eye on things.''

''I wish I could leave Barnabas or Tom to help you,'' said Captain Harken. ''But, as I said, we've got to obey orders. And Peran will back you up. So will the others.''

''Why has Captain James sent for Nicholas?'' asked Tom Gold.

''I don't know,'' said Captain Harken, ''but I think I can guess. Everyone in Ramir has heard the story of our voyage to the north, and how we were rescued by the People of the Snow, when we were lost on that ice-floe last year. The men were excited about it all, and the more they talked about it, the more the story grew.

''Captain James knows that Nicholas met the People of the Snow and helped them to rescue us. He may think that Nicholas knows more about them than even I do.''

Captain Harken looked rather grim for a moment. Then he smiled at Nicholas.

''Keep your courage up, Nicholas,'' he said. ''I'll see that no harm comes to you, you can be sure of that.''

Nicholas gulped and nodded. He always felt a little scared of Captain James.

"Well, there we are," said Captain Harken, pushing back his chair. "You'd better go back to the men, Downalong. Get them up on deck, and I'll have a word with them before we go across to *The Ice Queen*.

"The rest of you had better get your things together. Bring your ice clothes with you — the clothes we had among the icebergs in the far south. You'd better bring the clothes the snow people gave you, Nicholas. They're even warmer than ours. We leave in ten minutes."

Tom Gold, Barnabas and Nicholas were already dressed in warm woollen clothes from Ramir. While they packed their ice clothes into sacks, Captain Harken went on deck to speak to the men.

He told them simply that he was going over to *The Ice Queen* with Tom and Barnabas and Nicholas, and that Captain Cazzek would be taking over command of *The Snow Goose* for the time being, with Fryock and Garl. Downalong Joe was going to stay as boatswain. "If I send you any orders myself, I shall send them to Downalong Joe," he added. "If he's not here for any reason, then Peran will take over as boatswain."

Captain Harken said nothing more, and he gave no one a chance to ask questions.

The men were not looking very happy when the other three joined him on the deck. But the boat was lowered, and six buccaneers rowed them across to *The Ice Queen*.

Chapter 3
On *The Ice Queen*

Captain James was waiting for them.

"There are two starboard cabins off the great cabin on this ship," said Captain James, as they climbed on to the deck. "You will take one, Captain Harken. Brandy and Gold will share the other. The boy can swing a hammock below with the men."

"I'd rather have Nicholas in my cabin," said Captain Harken. "He's very useful, for carrying messages."

"I can't imagine that there will be any messages for him to carry on my ship," said Captain James coldly. "And a ship's boy doesn't have a cabin on deck, when I am in command."

"He's not a ship's boy," said Captain Harken quietly. "He's my adopted son."

"Your son!" cried Captain James. "You've adopted that boy as your son?"

"Yes," said Captain Harken, looking Captain James full in the face. "I adopted him on our voyage to the north last year. As you know, every captain in Ramir has the right to take members of his family with him, on board ship. I should like to have Nicholas with me."

Captain James shrugged his shoulders. "As you like," he said. "I trust you'll see that the boy does as he's told, and keeps out of my way."

He turned to one of the seamen, who was standing behind him.

"Bring up a sack of straw and some blankets for the boy," he said. "Put them in Captain Harken's cabin."

He turned back to Captain Harken.

"We'll take water on board here," he said. "We'll see if there's any food to be found on land, too. Then we shall sail north, to look for the Arcons."

They spent the rest of the day anchored off shore. Boats went to and fro, between the ships and the land, carrying barrels of water. They found blue-berries growing on shore, too. They found patches of the green plant which they called "scurvy grass", because it kept off scurvy. (Scurvy is the dreaded illness which sailors get, when they don't eat enough green food.) They brought great baskets of scurvy grass on board.

Nicholas would have liked to go ashore, but Captain James ignored him, and he didn't dare ask if he could go.

Everything seemed so different on *The Ice Queen*. Nicholas was thankful that he was in Captain Harken's cabin. He didn't know the buccaneers on *The Ice Queen,* but they didn't seem as friendly as the men on *The Snow Goose*.

They sailed that evening. Nicholas ate his supper at the big table in the great cabin with Captain Harken and the others, but it wasn't the same as the meals on *The Snow Goose*.

The food was richer. There was meat, and cheese made from goats' milk, and all kinds of sauces. There were tarts and biscuits to follow. Everyone was very polite, but no one said very much, except when Captain James asked a question. Even Captain Harken was silent.

But Nicholas slept well on his sack of straw that night. That was as comfortable as his bed on *The Snow Goose.* The cabin was larger, too, and Captain Harken didn't snore, like Barnabas Brandy.

Nicholas had had breakfast next morning, and was out on deck, when there was another cry from the cross-trees.

''There's a ship! An Arcon ship on the port bow!''

Captain Harken was up on the poop deck, with Captain James.

''Nip down to the cabin, and bring me my spy-glass, Nicholas,'' he called.

Nicholas ran to get it. By the time he had found it, and taken it up to Captain Harken, Captain James was already looking at the ship through his own telescope.

''It *is* an Arcon ship,'' he said. ''Is it the one you saw last year, Captain Harken?''

Captain Harken took the telescope that Nicholas handed to him, and trained it on the ship.

''Yes,'' he said. ''That's *The Fire-bird.* That's Ulf the Strong at the steering oar. They're our friends from last year.''

"I should hardly call a ship full of Arcons 'friends'," said Captain James coldly.

"We made a treaty of friendship with them," said Captain Harken. "We ate fish and salt together."

"So I have heard," said Captain James. "Well, at least that means that they will not attack us now."

"They'll welcome us to their homes," said Captain Harken. "They will want us to feast with them on shore tonight."

"Indeed?" said Captain James. "That may prove useful."

The two captains stood together on the poop deck, as the Arcons' ship sailed towards them.

"Francis! Francis Harken!" cried Ulf the Strong, as the ship came within hailing distance of *The Ice Queen,* and Ulf saw Captain Harken on the deck.

"Greetings, Ulf the Strong," Captain Harken called back.

The Arcon ship drew in close to *The Ice Queen.*

"What are you doing, here in the north?" cried Ulf, his deep voice booming out. "Is there more sickness in Ramir?"

"We have come in the hope of finding more snow-berries," said Captain Harken.

"Then you've come in the wrong year," boomed Ulf. "It was a late spring, and it will be an early winter. The ice is much farther south this year. You'll never reach the berry-fields this summer — or, if you do, you'll never get back. You have two ships now?''

"This is *The Ice Queen,* Ulf,'' called Captain Harken. "And this is Captain James, the High Captain of Ramir.''

"He is welcome, too, if he comes in peace,'' cried Ulf.

"Come aboard,'' shouted Captain James. "I should like to meet the leader of the Arcons.''

The Arcon ship drew alongside. A rope ladder was dropped over the side of *The Ice Queen,* and Ulf climbed on board.

"Welcome to our home in the north,'' he said to Captain James. He turned to Captain Harken. "I'm glad to see you again, Francis,'' he said. "We must have a feast tonight.''

Captain James looked at Ulf as if he were some strange animal. But he took him into the great cabin, and beckoned Captain Harken to go with them. A moment later, he opened the door again, and shouted to one of the seamen to bring a flask of wine.

"Well, that's a good beginning,'' said Barnabas Brandy, as he watched the door of the great cabin shut again. "Captain James looked as if he thought Ulf was a rat, caught stealing corn. But at least he took him into the cabin, and he's giving him wine.''

He was standing on the poop deck with Tom Gold and only Nicholas was near them.

35

Tom Gold shook his head.

"I don't trust him, Barnabas," he said in a low voice.

"Don't trust Ulf the Strong!" exclaimed Barnabas. "But he ate fish and salt with us!"

"That's not what I meant," said Tom Gold softly. "I trust Ulf the Strong. But you're right, when you say that Captain James looks at him as if he were a rat stealing corn. That's just how Captain James *would* think of an Arcon, up here near the berry-fields.

"I don't trust Captain James. And it's my belief that Captain Harken doesn't trust him, either."

"You're right there," said Barnabas Brandy. "He doesn't. It would take an earthquake to make Francis Harken go against the High Captain of Ramir. But I think there may be an earthquake — or something just as bad."

"So do I," said Tom Gold. He glanced at Nicholas. "I don't have to tell you to say nothing about this, Nick, do I?" he said.

"Of course not," said Nicholas.

"You can trust Nick till the mountains fall!" said Barnabas.

"I know that," said Tom Gold. "And so does Captain Harken."

The door of the great cabin opened, and the two captains came out with Ulf the Strong.

"Then we shall see you at the feast

tonight," said Ulf as he walked across the deck.

"You must let us bring a couple of barrels of wine with us," said Captain James.

Ulf laughed. "Wine is always welcome," he said. "We drank the last of the red wine you gave us at the mid-winter feast."

He glanced around him and saw Nicholas, who was still on the poop deck.

"So you've brought your son with you again, Francis," he cried. "Nicholas, isn't it? I didn't know you were here, boy. Hoon will be glad to hear it. He has a new boat, one of his own. He'll bring it across later, Nicholas, and take you fishing before the feast."

"I'd like that," said Nicholas. He remembered Hoon. He was a boy about his own age, and Nicholas had met him at last year's feast, when they had first met the North Arcons.

Ulf turned to Captain Harken.

"Will you let the boy go?" he asked. "He'll be safe with Hoon."

"Of course," said Captain Harken. "He'll enjoy it."

"Be sure that you bring him to the feast," said Ulf.

"I will," said Captain Harken with a smile.

Ulf turned to Captain James.

"When you sail into the bay this evening, we will set a marker for you, to show you the best place to anchor," he said. "The bay can be dangerous, if you don't know it. The marker is a ring of white wood."

"Thank you," said Captain James. "We will look for it."

Ulf climbed down into his ship, and waved his arm in farewell. The Arcons pulled away, towards the land.

As soon as they had gone, Captain James called to one of the seamen. The man came running.

"Send a signal to Captain Cazzek," he said. "Tell him to come over, and to bring Fryock with him."

The seaman ran up to the poop deck. He picked up two flags, and began to signal *The Snow Goose.*

Captain James turned to Captain Harken.

"We have plans to discuss," he said. "We will return to the great cabin."

He went back across the deck, and Captain Harken followed him.

A boat was lowered from *The Snow Goose.* Four buccaneers rowed it across, and in a few minutes Cazzek and Fryock climbed on board *The Ice Queen.* They went straight to the great cabin.

"There's something up," said Tom Gold softly.

Barnabas Brandy nodded. "I think so, too, Tom," he said. "You don't need to make plans, when you're going to a feast."

He thought for a moment.

"It may be that they're just deciding whether to try to sail north or not," he said. "We may have to give up the voyage, if the ice is as bad as Ulf said. But Captain James isn't the man to give up a voyage unless he has to, and I don't think he's talking about that — not yet."

"If it were that, he'd have called us in, too," said Tom Gold. "We were sailing *The Snow Goose* last year, when the ice came down from the north and Captain Harken was among the ice-floes. He'd want us there. We've learnt a lot about how to sail a ship through the ice.

"No. It's something else. I'm sure of that."

They went down to the main deck, and Nicholas stayed behind, watching the land and the sea.

A long way away, he could see a great iceberg sparkling in the sunshine. He stared out over the ship's side, thinking of the People of the Snow.

It was an hour before the door of the great cabin opened, and Captain James came out, with Cazzek and Fryock. Nicholas watched them go over to the ship's side, talking quietly.

Then Cazzek and Fryock climbed down into the boat, and the buccaneers rowed them back to *The Snow Goose*.

Captain James went back to the great cabin, and after a few minutes, Captain

Harken came on deck.

He saw Nicholas on the poop deck, and came up to join him.

"Hallo, Nick. You're looking very thoughtful," he said. "What are you thinking about?"

"I was thinking about the People of the Snow," said Nicholas.

"I might have guessed that," said Captain Harken.

He glanced around to make sure that they were alone.

"Ulf did say that Hoon would come over and take you fishing *before* we go to the feast this evening, didn't he?" he asked.

"Yes," said Nicholas. "I think that might be Hoon coming now."

He pointed across the water. A little boat with a red sail had come out of the bay, and was making for *The Ice Queen.*

"Good," said Captain Harken softly. "Now, listen very carefully, Nicholas. You must give Hoon a message for me. We are taking two barrels of wine with us to the feast tonight. One barrel will be of white wine, and one will be of red.

"Tell Hoon to tell Ulf that *none of the Arcons must drink the red wine.* And tell him that the message comes from me."

"But — the Arcons like red wine," said Nicholas. "They'd drink that first."

"I know," said Captain Harken. "And tonight the buccaneers would drink only the white. The red wine has been drugged, Nicholas. Captain James plans to make the Arcons his prisoners, and take over their houses.''

Nicholas stared at Captain Harken in dismay.

''But he can't!'' he exclaimed. ''They're our friends. We've eaten their fish and salt.''

''Sh!'' said Captain Harken. ''Speak softly, boy. You don't know who's listening.

''Soluken ordered Captain James to set up a base, here in the north. He plans to leave some of the buccaneers here when he sails for Ramir. He wants to leave one of the ships behind, too. They will either trade with the snow people, or take over the berry-fields themselves.

''The only place where they can stay through the winter is here, in the Arcons' houses. So Captain James wants to take over the village — and the sheep, too.

''It's because we made a treaty of friendship with the Arcons that I'm telling you this, Nicholas. I'm setting myself against the High Captain of Ramir. Captain James would think I was a traitor, if he ever learnt that I'd warned Ulf. And so would Soluken.

''But I'm not going to break that treaty of friendship, Nicholas, even though Captain James has ordered me to. I'm going to keep it, for the sake of the Arcons, and for the sake of Ramir. There are times when an order is so bad, that you mustn't carry it out. This is one of them.

"You'll tell Hoon?"

"Of course I'll tell him," said Nicholas.

Captain Harken smiled, and clapped him on the shoulder.

"We'll do the best we can to save the Arcons, Nick," he said. "And the men of Ramir, too. Here's your boat. Go off and have a few hours fishing. But don't be too long. Ask Hoon to bring you back to this ship, before we sail into the bay."

The little boat had drawn alongside *The Ice Queen*. Nicholas ran down to the main deck, and looked over the side. Hoon was sitting in it, holding on to the ship and grinning up at him cheerfully.

Nicholas waved, and climbed down to join him. The little boat pulled away from the ship's side.

Chapter 4
The Arcons' feast

Nicholas was back on *The Ice Queen* in time to sail into the bay. He had had a good afternoon's fishing with Hoon, and when he climbed back on board, he had a string of fish with him.

He saw Captain Harken standing on the deck, watching him as he came aboard. Nicholas gave him a quick nod, before he took the fish down to the cook.

The sun was low in the sky when *The Ice Queen* and *The Snow Goose* sailed slowly into the Arcons' bay.

They found a big ring of white wood floating on the sea, fastened to a rope, and guessed that this was the 'marker' Ulf had left for them. They anchored in front of the Arcons' houses.

The two ships of Ramir anchored near each other. Both ships lowered a boat. Ten men from *The Ice Queen,* and five from *The Snow Goose,* went ashore. Cazzek, Fryock and Garl were in the jolly boat from *The Snow Goose,* with Peran and Cass at the oars. Captain Harken and Nicholas went with Captain James and seven other buccaneers from *The Ice Queen.* They carried two casks of wine with them.

Ulf was waiting on the shore.

"Welcome once more," he said, as they got out, and the buccaneers pulled the boats up the beach. He spoke cheerfully, but Nicholas thought that his eyes were watchful.

He turned to Captain James.

"It is a custom in our country to eat fish and salt, as a sign of friendship," he said. "I ate the dish of friendship with Francis Harken last year, and he has proved a true friend.

"Now I will eat it with you, Captain James, before we take you to our homes."

He made a sign, and one of the Arcons handed him a dish with a piece of cooked fish on it. Another Arcon held out a shell full of salt.

Ulf took a pinch of salt, and scattered it on the fish. He took half the fish himself, and handed the other half to Captain James.

"Eat this, as a pledge of friendship between us," he said.

Captain James glanced quickly at Captain Harken, and then at Ulf. Then he put out his hand, took the fish, and ate it.

"Now there is friendship and peace between us," said Ulf.

Captain James made him a little, stiff bow.

"We have brought two casks of wine with us," he said. "In Ramir, we drink white wine, but I know that the Arcons like the red. So we have brought a cask of red wine and a cask of white, for the feast tonight."

Ulf looked at him. "You pledge your friendship in wine in Ramir?" he asked.

"Yes," said Captain James.

"Then we will drink your wine as a pledge

of friendship," said Ulf. He signed to some of the Arcons who were near him.

"Bring the casks up with you," he said. He turned back to Captain James. "We have made a hot drink of berries for you, but we will drink at least one of your casks of wine at our feast."

He turned, and led the way up to the houses of the Arcons.

Nicholas noticed that the Arcons had built another house since last year. Then, there had been three long houses in a row. Now there were four. The trapdoors in the grass-covered roofs were all open, and smoke was drifting up through them.

Nicholas took a deep breath of fresh air, and followed the others inside.

The house was just as he had remembered it. Low platforms lay along each wall, with sheepskin sleeping bags lying on them. There was a fire in the middle, under the trapdoor in the roof. He could see through the open doorways to the other houses beyond. There were black pots on the fires, and the smell of cooking drifted through.

They sat down on the platforms, among the Arcons, and the feast began.

First, the Arcons brought them horns full of the hot drink made from berries. It was rather like the drink Nicholas had tasted when he was with the People of the Snow. He was cold, and it warmed him.

But even without the drink, it would not

have been possible to stay cold for long. There were so many people crammed together along the platforms, and the glowing fire gave off such great heat, that Nicholas soon pulled off first his outer jacket, and then his under jacket, and sat on them.

Then the Arcons brought in great dishes of fish stew and meat stew and bowls of berries. Captain Harken had sent a message to Downalong Joe, to send barrels of flour and jars of honey from *The Snow Goose,* and these had been made into cakes. There was cheese made from goats' milk, and some kind of sour cream.

Nicholas couldn't eat a tenth of all the things they offered him.

Hoon made his way through the crowd, and squeezed in beside Nicholas.

"I told Ulf," he whispered. "But it must be all right now. Captain James ate the fish and salt on the shore."

"Don't trust him," Nicholas breathed in Hoon's ear. "Don't trust him, whatever he does."

"But if he breaks a promise, when it is made with fish and salt, he will die!" Hoon whispered back. "The gods of the seas and the mountains will not let him live! Doesn't he know that? Every Arcon knows that he will die, if he breaks a promise made with fish and salt."

"I don't think Captain James would believe that," said Nicholas. "But I don't know. Perhaps he's changed his mind. Perhaps he means to be friends, and that's why he took the fish and salt. But don't be too sure.''

''He must be friends now,'' said Hoon. ''He must be!''

''Will Ulf drink the red wine?'' asked Nicholas.

''We shall soon know,'' said Hoon. ''Look! Ulf is calling for the wine which you brought.''

Two of the Arcons brought in one of the casks of wine, and set it down on the floor in front of Ulf. Nicholas saw that it had already been opened.

Ulf got to his feet. The talk died down, and everyone listened.

''Captain James tells me that in Ramir you pledge friendship in wine,'' he said. ''And so we will drink your gift of wine together.''

He turned to Captain James, who was sitting beside him.

''We will save one cask of wine for your return, since you say that you must sail north,'' he said. ''We will have a great feast waiting for you, when you come back.

''We have opened the other cask, and we will drink it now, as a pledge of friendship.''

One of the Arcons handed him a big jug, made of silver. He dipped it into the open cask, and poured the wine into his drinking horn.

Nicholas gave a sigh of relief. It was the

white wine.

Ulf filled Captain James' drinking horn himself, and then handed the jug to one of the Arcons, and the wine was passed round. Nicholas took about a spoonful, put it in his drinking horn, and filled the horn up with water. When every horn was full, Ulf lifted his hand.

"I will drink first with Captain James, the High Captain of Ramir," he cried. "Captain James, let this wine be a sign of the friendship between us. And if any man drinks this wine, and breaks this pledge, then may the gods of the seas and the mountains take him!"

Ulf drained his drinking horn.

"This is the custom in Ramir," said Captain James.

He lifted his horn, and drank.

"The wine shall indeed be a sign between us," said Ulf, watching him. He filled his horn again, and turned to the others.

"Let the friends of the Arcons drink this wine!" he said.

Everyone lifted their horns and drank. Nicholas saw that Cazzek, Fryock and Garl were drinking with the others.

"They will never break their pledge of friendship now!" whispered Hoon.

"I hope not," said Nicholas.

He still didn't trust Captain James. The High Captain had eaten the fish and salt, and he had drunk the wine, but he had not promised friendship yet, in so many words.

Nicholas didn't want to talk about it any more, so he changed the subject.

"Why did you build another house?" he asked. "Have more Arcons come to join you?"

"We built the fourth house over a spring of water," said Hoon. "Now, if anyone attacks us, we can shelter in our houses. If we bar the doors, we shall still have water to drink. We've stored our food in the fourth house, too."

"Are you expecting someone to attack you?" asked Nicholas in surprise.

"After your ship came last year, we didn't feel safe," said Hoon. "You are our friends, we know that. But where one ship can come, so can another. And perhaps the next ship will not be so friendly."

Nicholas began to think that Ulf was not as easily taken in as Captain James had thought he would be.

"You can trust Captain Harken," he said.

"We all know that," said Hoon. "Captain Harken has kept his promise."

A great pie full of berries and topped with cream, was brought in, and the drinking horns were filled with wine once again.

When everyone had eaten as much as they could, one of the Arcons took out a harp, and began to sing.

Nicholas listened to the words of the song. It was the story of a man who had made a pledge of friendship, and then broken his

pledge for a sack of gold. He had given his friends away to his enemies.

The song told what happened then. That same night, a great snake had come up out of the sea, and swallowed him and the gold, too.

Nicholas looked at Captain James, to see how he was taking it. But Captain James was not even listening. He had drawn a map on the earth at his feet, and he was pointing to it. Nicholas heard him say something about ''a safe anchorage in the winter,'' and Ulf bent over the map to point one out to him.

There were more songs about the voyages of the Arcons, and more talk of the winter in the north. And then at last, when Nicholas's eyes were closing and he felt that he couldn't stay awake any longer, Captain James rose, and they started to go back to the ship.

Ulf went down to the shore with them.

''So you will sail in the morning?'' he said to Captain James. ''You cannot sail much farther north. As I told you, the ice has come far south this year. It has come so far south, that we have wondered if it has been sent by the People of the Snow, to drive us away. And indeed, if the winter is very bad this year, we may have to go.''

''We shall sail north as far as we can,'' said Captain James. ''If we can't reach the berry-fields by ship, we must go on foot over the ice.''

Ulf shook his head. ''It will be too dangerous,'' he said.

"The men of Ramir are not afraid," said Captain James coldly.

"Then they should be," said Ulf bluntly. "A wise man knows when to be afraid."

"Perhaps that is true for the Arcons," said Captain James. "It is not true for the buccaneers.

"But let us say nothing more about that. We have to thank you for your feast tonight, and for your help. I shall be glad to leave *The Snow Goose* behind. She can come to our rescue, if we run into danger farther north.

"I shall leave the ship here, under Captain Cazzek. We shall return, I hope, in a few weeks."

"You will have to return soon, if you want to sail back to Ramir this year," said Ulf. "Even here, the sea may freeze before long. Winter is coming early, and I think it will be even colder than last year."

"So you have said," said Captain James. "We shall be back as soon as we can. If the sea starts to freeze, *The Snow Goose* can wait for us in the mouth of the great river, to the south. You said that the sea doesn't freeze there."

"It has not frozen there before," said Ulf. "At least, not in any winter since we came to this north land. But perhaps even the river will freeze, if the winter is colder than before. Do not stay in the north too long."

"I shall remember your warning," said Captain James. "And now we must go."

He stepped into the boat.

"Goodbye, Ulf," said Captain Harken, holding out his hand. "The boatswain on *The Snow Goose* is Downalong Joe. Do you remember him? He was with me last year. He's a gloomy man, but he's a man you can trust."

Ulf looked at Captain Harken for a moment. Then he smiled.

"I remember him," he said. "If you trust him, so will I. Good luck go with you, Francis. You will have a hard voyage of it, sailing north."

"May good luck stay with you, Ulf," said Captain Harken.

He climbed into the boat. Nicholas said goodbye to Hoon, and followed them. The buccaneers pushed the boat off into the water and climbed in.

No one said anything at all, as they rowed back to *The Ice Queen*.

Chapter 5
Nicholas in trouble

The Ice Queen sailed the next morning, leaving *The Snow Goose* behind.

Nicholas stood on the deck with Barnabas Brandy and Tom Gold, looking back at the ship, and the Arcons' home, as they sailed out of the bay, and turned north.

"I wish Captain Harken had never agreed to sail on *The Ice Queen*," said Barnabas Brandy. "I'll be thankful when we're all back again on *The Snow Goose* — and still happier, when we're back in the Sea of Ramir, sailing on *The Silver Dolphin*!"

"I'll be glad to be back myself," said Tom Gold. "But an order is an order, Barnabas, and Captain James is in command."

Barnabas Brandy muttered something under his breath.

Nicholas left them, and went below to clear up the great cabin. Now that Captain James knew that Captain Harken had adopted Nicholas as his son, he gave him very little work to do in the ship. Captain Harken had asked Nicholas to look after their cabin, and to keep the great cabin clean and tidy, but when he had done that, he was free to do as he liked.

He spent most of his time on deck. He kept within sight of Captain Harken whenever he could, but much of the time he was on his own. Everyone was too busy working the ship, to talk to him.

The second day out from the Arcons' home, Nicholas saw a fog bank lying across the water ahead. He saw Captain Harken, who was on deck with Captain James, pointing to the fog. Captain James shook his head, and *The Ice Queen* continued under full sail. There was only a light breeze, but she was still sailing much faster than *The Snow Goose* had sailed into the fog.

That was the day when they first ran into real danger. Before they reached the fog bank they could see a field of ice, far over towards the east. The sea to the north and west was clear. When they entered the fog, Captain James sent a man to the cross-trees, and posted a look-out in the bows.

Nicholas was on the poop deck, and he heard Captain Harken say to Captain James: "The wind is swinging round to the south. We should change our course, and sail west — or north-west."

"If we do that, we shall be turning away from the berry-fields," said Captain James. "We shall reach them much more quickly if we sail due north, with a south wind behind us."

"But if we sail due north, we shan't be able to sail back the way we have come, if we find ice to the north and west of us, as well as to the east," said Captain Harken. "We can't sail south into the teeth of the wind. If we tack to the north-west, we can tack to the north-east later, and we shall still have a chance of turning back, if we have to."

"You seem to think of nothing but turning back," said Captain James. "My orders are to reach the berry-fields. I shall carry out those orders."

"It will be no use reaching the berry-fields, if we never return to Ramir with the berries," said Captain Harken quietly.

"I am in command of this ship, Captain Harken," said Captain James in a voice of cold fury. "You are here to advise me, because you have been here before. You are not here to argue with me. You did not wish to come, and it is my belief that you do not wish us to reach the berry-fields — or to get the scarlet berries at all.

"That makes your advice worthless. From now on, you will obey my orders, and you will only give advice when I ask for it."

Captain James turned on his heel, and left the poop deck. Captain Harken stood still, staring out into the fog. Nicholas didn't like to say anything to him. He stayed on deck, but he kept very quiet.

Half an hour later, Nicholas thought that the fog ahead of them seemed to be growing whiter. He was just going to ask Captain Harken about it, when the man in the cross-trees shouted: "Icebergs ahead! There's a berg on the port bow, and another to starboard!"

His voice rose. "They're moving together!" he cried. "We'll be crushed between them!"

Two great icebergs loomed out of the fog. Nicholas saw giant white cliffs of ice, and high pinnacles, like pointed towers. The water near the icebergs was pale green, above an island of ice in the sea below.

Captain Harken raced down to the wheel of the ship, and took over from the man standing there.

There was no time to turn to port or starboard. Their only chance was to sail through the gap in the icebergs, before the two great cliffs of ice closed.

Nicholas stared up at the icebergs, as the ship sailed in under them. Waves were breaking against them, and there was a swirl of white water ahead.

Captain Harken swung the wheel, and the ship slithered through the closing gap, turning a little to starboard. Her bowsprit just touched a pinnacle of ice that rose up on its own out of the sea, beyond the starboard iceberg. They felt her touch the side of the ice under the water, check, and slide along it, into the clear water beyond.

They were through the gap.

As they looked back into the thickening mist behind them, the gap between the two icebergs closed. Shattered pinnacles of ice fell down into the sea. Then the fog closed in, and they could see nothing more.

"Reef the main sail!" cried Captain Harken.

The buccaneers sprang to the rigging. Captain James came out of the great cabin.

Captain Harken gave up the wheel to the steersman, and walked over to join him.

"That was close," he said. "I hope we shall be out of the fog soon, but while we're in it, we should reef more sails. There are rafts of ice floating in the sea now. They look small, but any one of them could be the top of a great pillar of ice, reaching down under the water. If we strike something like that, the ice will smash in the bows of the ship. And we may reach the big fields of ice at any time."

Captain James had said that he didn't want any more advice, but he looked a little shaken.

"We shall still sail north, Captain Harken," he said. "and we shall take full advantage of the wind. The main sail may remain reefed for the time being — but not for long."

Nicholas found that his knees were trembling. He took a deep breath, and leant against the ship's side. *The Ice Queen* cut through the water, sailing due north.

The ship sailed out of the fog the next day. At one minute, there was a thick white blanket of fog all around them. In the next minute, it thinned to a blue mist, and a few moments later, *The Ice Queen* was sailing in sunshine under a blue sky.

"Ice ahead, and over on the starboard bow!" cried the man in the cross-trees.

Even from the deck, Nicholas could see a great ice field stretching over the sea. It lay across the water ahead of them, and over to their right, as far as they could see.

The water to the north-west seemed to be clear, and they altered course, sailing towards it. But as they sailed farther, they saw that here, too, the ice covered the sea to the north.

The Ice Queen sailed slowly on towards the edge of the ice field.

They had not yet reached it, when the evening meal was served in the great cabin. Captain James was at the head of the table. A buccaneer called Mallan, who was acting mate on *The Ice Queen,* was with him. Captain Harken was there, and so was Tom Gold. (Barnabas was on deck, in charge of the ship while the others ate.)

Nicholas always ate in the great cabin with Captain Harken, and he slipped into his place at the foot of the table.

"I have been reading the log of *The Snow Goose,*" said Captain James, as one of the buccaneers brought in plates of steaming food, and set them on the table. "That is, the log you made of your voyage last year.

"I see that, when you came to the ice field, you lowered a boat, and towed the ship through. And you found clear water on the far side."

"That's true," said Captain Harken.

61

"But that was last year. Ulf said that the ice is worse this year. There may be no clear water, beyond this ice field. Even if there is, the open lanes of water may freeze over, before we return."

Captain James lifted his goblet, and drank.

"So you would turn back?" he asked, holding it in his hand and looking at the wine.

"Yes," said Captain Harken.

"And what would you do then? Winter with the Arcons?"

Captain Harken shook his head. "I should sail south, until the spring," he said.

Captain James set his goblet down on the table.

"We shall not return to Ramir without the scarlet berries of the snow," he said.

Captain Harken said nothing.

"Well?" questioned Captain James sharply.

"We may have to, if we can't get through the ice," said Captain Harken quietly. "The berry-fields lie to the east of us. Last year, the clear water was to the east, and the ice was packed together in a great ice field to the west."

"You didn't get your berries from the berry-fields last year," said Captain James. "You got them from the People of the Snow. Perhaps we can do the same this year."

"Perhaps," said Captain Harken.

Captain James opened his mouth to speak, but he changed his mind, and shut it again.

They ate the rest of the meal in silence.

They were so far north now, that the sun didn't set, even at midnight. It hung low down in the sky, but it didn't drop quite below the horizon. Nicholas went into the starboard cabin to sleep for a few hours. He never knew what the time was. Day and night seemed to be much the same, and the buccaneers ate and slept without thinking about the time, as they sailed the ship north.

When he woke, and went on deck, Nicholas found that *The Ice Queen* had entered the ice field. They were making their way along a lane of clear water. One of the boats was out ahead, towing the ship. The sails had been furled, and there were great rafts and patches of ice all around them.

Tom Gold and Captain Harken were standing on the poop deck. Tom Gold was using Captain Harken's telescope. Nicholas ran up to the deck to join them.

Tom Gold handed the telescope back to Captain Harken.

"I think you're right," he said. "That dark cloud is over clear water. We'll get through this ice field into it. Captain James is lucky."

"I'm not so sure of that, Tom," said Captain Harken. "We may get through now. I hope we shall be able to get through, when we come back. But you'd better get down and report to Captain James. He's in the bows."

Tom Gold left the poop deck.

Captain Harken looked through the telescope again, and Captain James came up on to the poop deck to join him. Nicholas moved back out of the way. Captain James took no notice of him, but Nicholas never felt comfortable when he was there.

"So you think there's clear water ahead?" asked Captain James.

Captain Harken nodded.

"Yes," he said. "Do you see the dark clouds to the north?"

"Well?" asked Captain James.

"The clouds are dark over clear water," said Captain Harken. "If you look to the east, you'll see white light shining on the clouds. That's not the sun breaking through. That's white ice on the sea, shining up on to the dark clouds overhead. The clouds are almost like a mirror, showing the ice below."

"But it's clear to the north," said Captain James.

"It's clear at the moment," said Captain Harken. "We don't know for how long it will stay clear. And we shall have to turn east before long, to reach the berry-fields. There is ice over there to the east, as far as we can see. There's fog coming in the north, too. The cloud is moving down."

Captain James turned and looked at Nicholas. His eyes looked so hard and fierce, that Nicholas felt his knees shaking.

Then he turned to Captain Harken.

"I think the time has come for us to discuss matters," he said. "Come down to the great cabin."

They left the poop deck together. Nicholas stared after them. He felt very uneasy.

As the two captains went into the great cabin, Nicholas saw Captain James beckon one of the buccaneers to come to him. He stopped for a moment to send the man below, and then went inside.

A few minutes later, the man returned with Mallan, the acting mate, and the boatswain, whose name was Krekil. They both went into the great cabin, and the door shut behind them.

Nicholas stared out over the sea, but he wasn't really watching, as the boat towed *The Ice Queen* from one open lane of water to the next. He was wondering what was going on in the cabin. He remembered the look Captain James had given him, and wondered if he had done anything to anger him.

Nicholas was not surprised when a buccaneer came up on to the poop deck half an hour later, and told him that Captain James wanted to see him.

His hands shook a little, as he ran down the steps, and across the deck to the door of the great cabin, but he went as quickly as he could.

He opened the door and went inside. He threw back the hood of his parka, pulled off his mitts, and pushed them into his pockets.

Captain James was sitting at the head of the table. Mallan and Krekil were sitting on either side of him. Captain Harken was next to Krekil, on Captain James' left.

Nicholas shut the door behind him, and stood still, facing Captain James.

There was a moment's silence, while Captain James stared at him, with the same fierce, hard stare. Then he spoke.

"I think you can help us, Nicholas," he said. "You were left behind in the berry-fields last year, weren't you?"

Nicholas nodded. "Yes," he said. His mouth felt dry, and he spoke almost in a whisper.

"Speak up, boy!" commanded Captain James.

"Yes, I — I was left behind in the fog," he said, rather more loudly.

"And you found Hornwollen? Hornwollen the traveller, who came here from Ramir, years ago?"

"Yes," said Nicholas. His thoughts went back to the old man. Nicholas had saved him from a bear, and Hornwollen had taken him to the rock castles, where the People of the Snow lived.

"Hornwollen lives here now?" asked Captain James.

"He — he did, last year," said Nicholas. "I don't know if he's here now."

"What happened after you found him?" demanded Captain James.

"Hornwollen took me to the People of the Snow," said Nicholas. "They went to look for Captain Harken, and they took me with them. They found Captain Harken on an ice-floe."

"Where did *Hornwollen* take you?" asked Captain James.

"I don't understand," said Nicholas.

"It's very simple," said Captain James. "You didn't meet the People of the Snow in the middle of the ice, did you?"

Nicholas shook his head.

"Then where did you meet them?" asked Captain James.

Nicholas glanced at Captain Harken. Captain Harken was staring down at the table.

"I — I met them where they live," said Nicholas.

"Now we have it!" said Captain James. "You met them where they live! So you know where to find the People of the Snow. You know where their home is."

Nicholas shook his head.

"I couldn't find my way there," he said. "There was snow and fog — and we moved about among the ice. I couldn't find my way back."

"I can understand that," said Captain James. "But there, I think, Captain Harken's log will help us. We know where-abouts the People of the Snow must live. But we do not know what to look for.

"You are wearing the white clothes they gave you?"

Nicholas nodded. He always put on the white trousers and parka and boots when he went on deck, because they were so warm.

"Their houses may be white, too, and difficult to see. I want you to tell us exactly what they look like, and where they are.

"I see from the log that there was an island to the west of the berry-fields, and there were great cliffs on the coast. Were the houses anywhere near there?"

Nicholas stared at Captain James, but he said nothing.

"Well?" barked Captain James suddenly.

Nicholas pulled himself together.

"I — I can't tell you where the People of the Snow live," he said unhappily. "I promised not to. They saved my life, and they saved Captain Harken and the others, too. And all they asked in return, was that I would promise never to tell anyone where they lived. Not even Captain Harken. And I promised.

"I've never told anyone anything about their houses. And — and I'm very sorry, but I can't tell you."

"So you've found your tongue at last," said Captain James, sitting back in his chair. "And now you've decided to speak, you refuse to answer my questions! You — a boy from no one knows where!"

He looked Nicholas up and down.

"This is an order," he said, slowly and clearly. "Answer my question. Tell me where the People of the Snow live."

"I can't," said Nicholas. "I promised."

"You can't ask the boy to break his promise, Captain James," Captain Harken broke in. "He owes his life to the People of the Snow. So do I. All they asked of us, was that they should be left alone.

"I have come with you to find the berry-fields, because the Council of Ramir ordered me to. But — "

Captain James turned on him before he could finish.

"I can see why the boy is so obstinate," he said. "He does what you tell him."

"I wasn't there when he gave his word to the People of the Snow," said Captain Harken quietly. "But I have always encouraged him to keep his word — yes."

"And encouraged him to disobey orders," said Captain James. "Nicholas, either you answer my question, or I shall look on you as a mutineer, and dismiss you from my ship."

"You can't do that!" cried Captain Harken.

"I not only can, but I will," said Captain James. "Either you answer my question, Nicholas, or we shall put you down on the ice field, and leave you there."

"But the boy will die in the cold!" said Captain Harken.

"I shall leave three days' food with him,"

said Captain James. "Perhaps his friends, the People of the Snow, will find him. In any case, you will leave this to me, Captain Harken. Unless, perhaps, you will tell him to obey me?"

"I can't do that," said Captain Harken. "Not when you are ordering him to break his word."

"Well, Nicholas?" said Captain James.

Nicholas said nothing. He just shook his head.

"I mean what I say, Nicholas," said Captain James. "If you refuse to answer my questions, you will be left on the ice. You understand that?"

Nicholas nodded miserably.

"And you still refuse?"

"I can't tell you," said Nicholas.

"Very well," said Captain James. "Krekil!"

"Just a moment," said Captain Harken. "You remember that Nicholas is now my son, Captain James. You have no right to take the boy from me, unless I agree. That is the law of Ramir. And I will not agree to this."

Captain James turned on him.

"You will agree, Captain Harken," he barked. "I order you to agree."

Captain Harken shook his head. "That is not the law of Ramir," he said. "I have to agree freely, of my own will. Unless I do, you have no right to part me from my son."

Captain James' face grew red.

"If you do not agree," he said. "I will not part you from your son. I shall leave you behind on the ice with him. That is how we treat mutineers on this ship, Captain Harken."

"I am no mutineer, Captain James," said Captain Harken quietly. "It is you who are breaking the law."

"Will you agree?" shouted Captain James in a sudden rage.

"I will never agree to leaving Nicholas behind," said Captain Harken.

"Then you will join him on the ice. Krekil!"

Krekil pushed back his chair, and got to his feet.

"Go out on deck," ordered Captain James. "Bring the ship in against the edge of the ice, and anchor her fore and aft, for a few minutes. Send below for a bag of food — enough for two men for three days."

He turned to Captain Harken.

"The boy is in his ice clothes. Go and get into yours," he said.

Captain Harken went into his cabin without a word.

Captain James stared at Nicholas.

"You see what you are doing?" he said. He spoke quietly, so that Captain Harken would not hear. But every word dropped out of his mouth, like stones dropping into a pool. "If Captain Harken freezes to death on the ice, it will be your fault — unless you want to change your mind?"

"I — I don't know," said Nicholas. His mouth felt dry. He swallowed hard. His head seemed to be whirling round. "I don't know what to do. I promised the snow people. They saved our lives."

He stared at Captain James.

"You could save yourself, and Captain Harken too, by telling me all you know," said Captain James. "And you would only be obeying orders. You have to obey the orders of the captain of your ship. I am High Captain of Ramir. I have ordered you to tell me."

"But I promised not to tell even Captain Harken," said Nicholas.

"You had no right to make that promise," said Captain James angrily. "You have no right now to keep it."

"But — but —" stammered Nicholas.

The door of the starboard cabin opened, and Captain Harken came back into the room. He was dressed in the clothes made of skins, which he had worn when they had been among the icebergs of the far south.

He looked quickly from Nicholas to Captain James.

"You haven't told him, Nick, have you?" he asked.

Nicholas shook his head.

"Did he tell you that you could save me by telling him?"

"Yes," gulped Nicholas.

"Don't you believe it," said Captain Harken. "We'll be left behind anyway, now. You keep your word to the People of the Snow."

Captain James brought his fist down on the table with a crash. His face was red with fury.

"Mutiny!" he cried. "Mutiny! Now I see why the boy is so obstinate! So that is the way you bring up your son, Captain Harken! You teach him to disobey orders.

"I didn't want to have you with me on this voyage. The Council of Ramir insisted, because you have been here before. They were wrong.

"Well, you have chosen your own path. Come!"

He stormed out on deck.

Captain Harken smiled at Nicholas. "Keep your courage up, Nick," he said. "We're in this together."

They went out on deck.

Krekil was waiting there, with a small bag in his hand. Six other buccaneers stood behind him.

The Ice Queen was anchored fore and aft to a great island of ice, at the west side of the open channel of water. A rope ladder hung down over the side of the ship.

Krekil handed the bag to Captain Harken.

"That's your food," he said.

"What's happening?"

Nicholas heard Barnabas Brandy's voice

from the poop deck. He looked up, and saw Barnabas and Tom Gold standing there, looking down on them.

"Get ashore!" commanded Captain James.

Captain Harken tossed the bag of food over the side on to the ice. Then he climbed quietly over the ship's side, and down the rope ladder.

Nicholas followed him. As he stepped down on to the ice he stumbled. Captain Harken gripped his arm, and pulled him quickly away from the edge of the water.

There were two buccaneers already on the ice, waiting for them. As soon as Nicholas had landed safely, Krekil called out an order. The buccaneers pulled up the anchors holding the ship, and climbed back on board.

The jolly boat took the tow rope again, and began to tow *The Ice Queen* on, down the lane of clear water.

Nicholas saw Barnabas Brandy and Tom Gold gazing at them from the poop deck. He could see the shock and anxiety on their faces.

He stood beside Captain Harken watching *The Ice Queen,* until she disappeared into a bank of white fog, which lay across the ice and the sea.

Chapter 6
The second mutiny

Barnabas Brandy and Tom Gold stood on the poop deck of *The Ice Queen*, looking back at the two figures left on the ice. They watched until the fog rolled over them, and they could see nothing more.

"What in all the seas has happened now?" said Barnabas Brandy.

"I don't know," said Tom Gold. "But I don't like it."

"He can't have left them behind!" exclaimed Barnabas.

"It looks very much like it," said Tom Gold. "I'm going to find out. There's only one way to do that, and that is to go and ask him."

"I'll go," said Barnabas, starting towards the steps.

"No, you won't," said Tom Gold, catching him by the arm, and holding him back. "You'd get so angry that you'd explode, and then we wouldn't find out anything. Leave this to me."

Barnabas hesitated for a moment, and then nodded.

"All right, Tom," he said. "You've a cooler head than I have. See what you can do. But if you need any help, give a shout, and I'll be with you in a brace of shakes!"

"You wait here, Barnabas," said Tom, clapping him on the shoulder. "I'll be back."

He went down on to the deck, and into the great cabin.

Captain James was sitting at the table, reading the old log of *The Snow Goose*. He looked up as Tom Gold came in.

"Well?" he barked.

"I'm worried about Captain Harken, Captain," said Tom Gold quietly. "You'll remember that I'm one of his men, from *The Snow Goose*.

"Can you tell me when he'll be returning to *The Ice Queen*?"

Captain James drew in his breath, and for a moment Tom Gold thought he was going to be ordered out of the cabin.

But then Captain James settled himself back in the chair, and looked him up and down, as if he were trying to make up his mind about something.

"I'm not used to men questioning what I do on this ship," he said at last. "If you were one of my own men, I should order you up to the cross-trees for twenty-four hours, as a punishment. But I know that Captain Harken treats his men differently.

"You are wondering why we have left Captain Harken behind?"

Tom Gold nodded. "Yes, Captain," he said.

"Very well. I like to see a man who is loyal to his captain — any captain. Just remember that I am the High Captain of Ramir. You owe a greater loyalty to me, than you do to

Captain Harken.

"You have sailed in the north before, and I may need your help, in working the ship through the ice. I will tell you why we have left Captain Harken behind.

"We have left him, so that he can show us the way to the People of the Snow."

"I don't understand," said Tom Gold.

"You know that the boy, Nicholas, was taken to the home of the People of the Snow, when you were here last year?" asked Captain James.

"He never said so," said Tom Gold. "But I've always thought he might have been."

"The boy knows where the People of the Snow live," said Captain James. "He admits as much, but he refuses to tell me anything about them.

"I have left him on the ice, because I am sure that he will lead us to them. Either they will come for him, or he will go to them.

"Captain Harken refused to tell me where to find them. It's possible that the boy hasn't told even Captain Harken where they live."

"I'm sure he hasn't," said Tom Gold.

"Perhaps not," said Captain James. "I'm not as sure as you are. But in any case Captain Harken has refused to make him tell me.

"So I have left Captain Harken on the ice, too, with the boy. Captain Harken will see that the boy comes to no harm, until the People of the Snow arrive.

"We shall sail north for another two or three hours. Then we shall anchor.

"In two days time, we shall return the way we have come. Either we shall find the People of the Snow rescuing Captain Harken and the boy, or we shall find their tracks. I have been studying Captain Harken's log, and I am certain that we are close to their home. We can follow their tracks to it.

"Then we shall buy the scarlet berries of the snow from them, if they will sell them. Or we shall take the berries by force, if they won't. And so we shall do what we were ordered to do by the Council of Ramir.

"I have told you this, Tom Gold, because I can see that you are loyal to your captain, and because I don't want you to do anything stupid. You may tell Barnabas Brandy, but no one else. That is an order. Do you understand?"

"I understand," said Tom Gold. "But I must tell you, Captain James, that what you're trying to do isn't possible.

"You have seen the sea and the ice. We're moving north through an open lane of water, towed by the jolly boat. That lane of water can close up at any time. The ice is moving with the current, and I think there's a storm coming. We may never get back through this ice field. If we do get back, it may be through an opening in the ice miles away. Every metre that we sail, gives us less chance of

returning to find Captain Harken and Nicholas.''

He glanced at the window.

''Look at the fog!'' he said. ''It's rolled down over us. If we go on through this fog, we shall never find our way back the way we came. A lane of water isn't like a road. It opens and closes in the ice.

''There may be bears on the ice, too. What chance have they got, if a bear attacks them?''

Captain James looked out of the window.

''The fog is thick enough to hide us from the snow people, when they come to rescue the boy,'' he said. ''I'll grant you that. Very well. We'll anchor to the ice here, and wait for the fog to lift. I think the People of the Snow may be here by that time.

''As for the bears — the boy scared one off before. Captain Harken put that down in the log. The boy blew his horn, and the bear ran away.

''Nicholas has the horn with him. It's always round his neck. If a bear attacks them, they can scare it away again.

''No, Gold. I've no fears for Captain Harken and the boy. I'm only afraid that they may get away in this fog, without us seeing where they go. Perhaps it would be wiser to stay closer to them.''

Captain James got up and walked over to the door of the great cabin. He opened it, and looked out.

"Krekil!" he shouted.

"Aye, aye, Captain!"

"Tell Mallan to anchor the ship fore and aft to the ice, on the east side of the channel.

"I'm going to take a watch below. Call me if you see anything at all. And in any case, call me as soon as the fog lifts."

"Aye, aye, Captain," said Krekil.

Captain James turned to Tom Gold. "It's a long time since I've had any sleep," he said. "I'm going to my cabin now.

"You will go on deck, and bring Barnabas Brandy down to your cabin. You will tell him what I have told you. You will tell no one else, and you will both stay in your cabin, until I send you word.

"Is that understood?"

"It is understood, Captain," said Tom Gold quietly.

Captain James nodded. "Very well," he said. "Go and get Brandy."

He was still standing in the great cabin, when Tom Gold returned from the deck with Barnabas. He watched the two of them go into their cabin. Then he turned, straightened his shoulders, and went into his own. As soon as he had shut the door, he almost stumbled. He hadn't slept for three nights, and now that he was alone, he could show how tired he was.

Captain James flung himself down on to his bunk, and fell asleep.

* * *

In their little starboard cabin, Barnabas was staring at Tom Gold.

"But he's mad!" cried Barnabas. "Captain James has gone mad! How in all the seas does he think we're going to get back down this channel? Doesn't he know that the wind is getting up? Doesn't he know that the ice shifts about in the current? That channels of clear water open and close all the time?"

"Keep your voice down, Barnabas," said Tom Gold quietly. "I tried to tell him. That's why he's anchored now."

"That won't do any good, if we stay here till the fog lifts!" said Barnabas. "Anything can happen in an hour — or in a few minutes! By the time the fog lifts, we won't be able to get back, even if we want to."

"But it gives us a chance to get a boat back now if we start right away," said Tom Gold softly.

"Now you're talking sense," said Barnabas Brandy.

"Then listen to me for a minute," said Tom Gold. "Captain James' men don't ask questions. He told me so, and I believe him.

"He's dead tired. I could see that, when he was talking to me. He'll be asleep now.

"We'll change into our ice clothes, and go on deck. I'll order the men to lower that small boat in the stern, and you go down to the galley, and bring up what food you can.

"If the men think anything about it at all, they'll think that it's all part of Captain

82

James' plan. He's put Captain Harken and Nick on the ice. They don't know why. Krekil may know, but he won't have told anyone. I saw him go below as I came down.

"Mallan's down on the ice, checking the anchors. They'll think we've been sent on to the ice for some reason, too.

"We'll simply take the boat, and find our way back to Captain Harken."

"We'll never find them in this fog," said Barnabas.

"Yes, we will," said Tom Gold. "I've got one of the horns from The Strange Land. So have they. We'll blow it when we're well clear of the ship. They'll hear us, and answer."

"You're right, Tom," said Barnabas. "We'll find them. But why don't we take the jolly boat? That's in the water now."

Tom Gold shook his head.

"*The Ice Queen* needs the jolly boat, to tow her through the ice fields," he said. "Captain James would be lost without it. Captain Harken would never take the jolly boat. He'd send us back with it.

"But if we've got the small boat, he'll use it to try to get back to the Arcons and *The Snow Goose*."

"You've got brains, Tom," said Barnabas. "I'll say that for you. Let's get our ice clothes on."

They changed quickly into their ice clothes. Tom Gold slung his horn around his neck.

"Let's take the blankets, too, Tom," said Barnabas, when they were ready.

"Good idea," said Tom Gold. "Bundle them up. And I'll make sure that there's a sail in the small boat."

They made their blankets into two big bundles, and tied them with rope.

Then Tom Gold opened the door, and looked out into the great cabin. It was empty. Captain James had been too tired to think of setting a guard. It had not entered his head that Tom and Barnabas might disobey his orders.

Tom took the two bundles of blankets. Barnabas went below to the galley, and Tom went to the bows of the ship. He ordered four seamen to lower the small boat into the water. They obeyed him without question. He dropped a rope ladder over the side.

Barnabas appeared with a sack of food, and an axe slung over his shoulder.

"I thought this might be useful," he said.

Tom Gold nodded. "Good man," he muttered. "We can use that to chop ice — or tackle bears!"

Barnabas climbed down into the boat, and Tom lowered first the sack, and then the two bundles, down to him.

Tom climbed down into the boat himself. The seamen stood watching, but they didn't seem very interested in what was happening.

They saw Mallan out on the ice with two of the men. They were shifting one of the anchors. Mallan scarcely glanced at them.

No one questioned orders, on *The Ice Queen*.

Tom and Barnabas stowed the sack and the bundles of blankets in the bows and stern of the boat. Tom checked that there was a mast and a sail. Then they each took an oar, and pulled away into the fog.

Chapter 7
The blizzard

Before the fog came down, Captain Harken and Nicholas found a small ice cave. They had crossed the island of ice, and discovered that there was sea all around it, so that they couldn't leave it. So Captain Harken had said that they must find what shelter they could.

"There's a change coming in the weather, Nicholas," he said. "There will be fog soon, but the wind's getting up. I shouldn't be surprised if we have snow. The clouds are dark and heavy. In fact, this time that fog is just a thick cloud resting on the sea."

They found the little cave in a large rock of ice in the centre of the island. Captain Harken took the food out of the sack, and stacked it at the back of the cave. He spread the sack on the ice, for them to sit on.

"It's not much, Nicholas," he said. "But it's better than nothing. And I've got something better still."

He pulled a little bundle out from under his skin jacket, and unwrapped it. It was a metal box. Inside the box was the little stove which the People of the Snow had given him a year ago, when they took the buccaneers back to *The Snow Goose*.

"Do you remember this? This will keep us warm," Captain Harken said cheerfully.

He opened the metal box. He took out the

stove, and set it down. The lid and bottom of the box made two pots, for cooking.

Captain Harken pulled a little black lever, and fitted the rings of bright metal together carefully. At once, they began to glow with a silvery light, and Nicholas felt the warmth on his face.

"When the sea freezes a bit more, we'll make our way across the ice field to the shore on the west, Nick," said Captain Harken. "And then we'll turn south, for the homes of the Arcons. I think it's all one land, over there to the west, and the Arcons are on the south tip of it."

"We've only got food for three days," said Nicholas.

"We'll make it last a bit longer than that," said Captain Harken. "I brought something else with me, too."

He pulled out a long fishing line and some hooks from an inside pocket.

"We might try a bit of fishing now," he said, "before the fog comes. It's no use sitting here, and waiting for the snow. I think there may be a storm coming, but it's not here yet. Let's see if we can add to our food supply, before it arrives."

They left everything except the fishing lines in the cave, and went across the ice to a place at the edge of the island, where the ice was thick and firm right up to the water.

Captain Harken marked the ice as they

went, so that they could find their way back to the cave, even in a fog.

The fishing was good. When at last the fog rolled slowly over them, they had caught five big fish.

They took the fish with them, and went back to the cave.

Nicholas couldn't help feeling happy, as he sat down on the sack by the little stove, and helped Captain Harken to cook the fish. They were on an island of ice, in the middle of a sea that would soon freeze. The fog had come down, and a storm was coming. They were alone, with no one to help them. And yet Nicholas felt happier than he had felt for a long time.

Captain Harken cooked one of the fish, and left the others on the ice at the back of the cave.

"There's one thing about this place," he said. "You don't have to worry about keeping food. You just put it on the ice, and it freezes. We shan't run out of food, while we can fish, Nick."

By the time they had finished eating, the wind was rising, and the fog was blowing away in the wind.

But as the fog lifted, the snow began to fall. At first, there were only a few flakes, blowing across the mouth of the cave. But soon the air was full of it, and they could see nothing but driving snow.

"It's a good thing the wind's from the

south-west, and the cave faces north," said Captain Harken. "I wish we'd got something to cover the entrance."

"What will happen to the ice, in this wind?" asked Nicholas.

"It will depend on the current," said Captain Harken. "The wind is driving it north-east, but the current runs south. I don't know quite what will happen, Nick. We shall have to wait and see."

Nicholas stared out into the driving snow.

"I wonder when we'll see Barnabas and Tom Gold again," he said. "I wonder what's happening to *The Ice Queen*."

"It's difficult to say," said Captain Harken. "The lanes of open water will close and change, as the ice drifts in the wind and current."

A horn sounded faintly across the ice.

Captain Harken leapt to his feet.

"That's a horn from The Strange Land!" he cried. "It's either the snow people — or it's Barnabas and Tom Gold here now!"

He pulled out his own horn, stepped to the entrance of the cave, and blew.

The sound echoed away into the driving snow.

As they listened, the first horn sounded again.

"Have you got your horn with you, Nick?" asked Captain Harken.

"Yes," said Nicholas, pulling it out from under his parka.

"You stay here. Count five hundred, and blow your horn. Then count another five hundred, and blow again. Go on like that till we're back. I'll go out towards whoever is coming, and guide them back here. There's a real blizzard blowing outside."

He stepped outside, and was gone, hidden by the snow.

Nicholas counted five hundred, and blew his horn. He counted another five hundred, and blew again. This time, he heard another horn answer him. It was nearer now.

He counted again, and blew.

A few minutes later, three figures, coated with snow and each carrying a heavy bundle, staggered to the mouth of the cave.

One by one, they shook the snow from their clothes, and came inside.

"Well, Nick, I hope you've got supper ready!" said Barnabas Brandy, dropping his bundle.

His beard and eyebrows were thick with ice, but his voice sounded as cheerful as ever.

"I'll get it," said Nicholas.

"Give us time to get in," said Captain Harken. "Tom, help me fix this sail across the mouth of the cave. We'll spread the blankets out later."

"It feels warm enough in here, after that boat," said Tom Gold. "I didn't know you'd brought the stove with you. I might have guessed. I'd forgotten you had that.

"How are you, Nick? I'm glad to see you, boy!"

"I'm fine," said Nicholas. "Did you come in the jolly boat?"

"In the small boat," said Tom Gold. "We've left her hauled up on the ice. Had we better drag her over here, Captain, before we settle in?"

"If you think that you've still got the strength to go out again, we will," said Captain Harken. "It'll be safer, and we can use the boat for shelter."

"Let's try," said Barnabas. "Tom and I are all right. We're buccaneers. You get that supper on, Nick, and blow your horn from time to time. The snow's thicker than a fog out there."

The three of them went out again into the snow.

Nicholas put another fish on to cook in the top of the metal box which had held the stove, and he put a big lump of ice in the bottom half. The men would want something hot to drink, when they got back.

It took the three buccaneers another half hour to drag the small boat over the ice to the cave, but they managed it.

They set the boat upside down on six blocks of ice across the entrance.

"That'll help to keep the snow out, if the wind changes," said Captain Harken.

They cut more blocks of ice, to fill the entrance to the cave. They left only a small hole under the boat, where they could climb in and out.

The fish was cooked and the water was boiling long before they had finished. But they didn't stop until everything was done, and Nicholas kept the fish warm for them. He cooked some dried meat, too.

Barnabas and Tom Gold ate the fish, and then they all shared the meat, and the hot drink, which Nicholas made by pouring the boiling water over some dried berries. (They all had their drinking horns with them.)

"Captain James is in for a surprise, when he finds we've gone," said Barnabas Brandy, sitting back and holding his drinking horn in both hands.

"So he was planning to come back for us," said Captain Harken thoughtfully. Tom Gold had told him everything that had happened.

"That's what he said," answered Tom Gold. "I can't be sure, but I think he told me the truth. I think he was angry with Nick, but he was acting a bit, perhaps. He wanted to make Nick think that his life depended on his finding the snow people. Your life, too, Captain. He was sure Nick would go to them, if *The Ice Queen* sailed off, leaving you both on the ice."

"I can't go to them," said Nicholas. "I don't know where they are. I could never find them, in all this ice and snow."

"Nobody's asking you to go to them, Nicholas," said Captain Harken. "We're not even going to try to find them. We'll make our way south, back to the Arcons and *The Snow Goose.* I think we could go over the land. The sea will freeze right across to the shore before long.

"But now that we've got a boat, we'll go by water where we can, and pull it over the ice where we can't. I think we've still time to get through. But if we haven't, we'll make the sail into a tent, and go south along the shore."

Barnabas Brandy laughed.

"I can't tell you how glad I am to be back with you as captain again, Francis," he said. "I had had just about as much as I could stand, of Captain James and *The Ice Queen.*"

"What happens when we get back to *The Snow Goose*?" asked Tom Gold. "Do we sail back to Ramir?"

"Why not?" cried Barnabas. "The Council of Ramir will never support Captain James — not after this."

"It's not the Council of Ramir I'm thinking about," said Tom Gold. "It's Soluken."

"You may be right, Tom," said Captain Harken. "While Soluken is regent, we shall have to be careful.

"But don't let's think about that now. For the time being, we must think about nothing but how best to get back to *The Snow Goose.*

"We can't do anything at the moment. There's a blizzard raging outside. So we'll rest. You must be exhausted, after that journey in the boat. I'm tired myself, hauling it over the ice, and Nick looks as if he could do with some sleep, too.

"Share out those blankets. We'll sleep for a while. We shall be able to plan things better when we've rested."

Barnabas and Tom Gold undid the blankets. They spread one over the floor, and handed out four others.

The ice was hard, and the walls of the cave dripped a little, from the warmth of the stove. But a few minutes later they were all asleep.

Chapter 8
Across the ice

The blizzard raged for three days. Captain Harken and the others stayed in the cave, while the snow drove past in the gale.

The wind shifted, and covered the boat and the entrance to the cave with a deep drift of snow. They had to tunnel a way through it, to get fresh air.

Then the wind changed again. It was difficult to tell which way it was blowing, because the island of ice moved and swung on the sea. But Captain Harken thought it was blowing from the east.

"I hope it does blow us close to the western shores," he said. "There's land to the west, and land to the east. But the Arcons live to the south and west of us, so we should go west, if we have to travel over land."

Barnabas and Tom Gold had been able to bring some food with them, but they didn't know how long it would have to last. They were very careful with it, and Nicholas felt hungry most of the time.

The little stove kept them warm. Captain Harken found that he could alter the amount of heat it gave out, by pulling on the little black lever on the side. They made it really hot for cooking, and the rest of the time they kept it warm enough to keep them fairly comfortable in their thick clothes. If they made it too warm, the ice roof of the cave dripped on them. The stove gave out a silvery light all the time, so that they were never in the dark.

When they woke on the morning of the fourth day, everything was silent outside. (They called it "morning", but they couldn't tell, inside the cave, whether it was night or day.)

They crawled out through the little tunnel they had made under the boat, and gazed around them. There was no sign of *The Ice Queen*.

There was no wind. The sun was shining down from a blue sky. To the north and west and east, they could see nothing but a great field of ice, stretching across the water. Beyond the ice, they could see the hills and cliffs of the land.

Half a mile away, there was still clear water to the south of them. They could see great icebergs floating in it, and rafts of ice, which had broken away from the rest. But there was plenty of room between them for a boat to sail south.

"There's a bear on the ice," said Tom Gold suddenly, pointing west.

They looked, and saw a great yellow-white bear, standing on the ice field half a mile away. He was looking towards them.

"Blow your horn, if he comes this way, Nicholas," said Captain Harken, pulling his pistol out of his belt.

The bear had seen them. He stood quite still, gazing at them, for about five minutes.

Then he turned, and clambered down over the ice towards the sea. As they watched, he came to the open water. He pushed himself off from the edge of the ice, and swam away in the sea.

"He's gone fishing," said Barnabas.

"We'd better fish, too, while we can," said Captain Harken. "We'll need more food for the journey south, and we must fish while the weather is fine.

"But with bears about, no one should go alone. You and Tom stay here and guard the cave, Barnabas. The bears might smell our food, and come here for it. Nicholas and I will go fishing. We shan't go far — just to the edge of the ice."

"Where's the ship?" asked Tom Gold.

"Who knows?" said Captain Harken. "She could have been blown anywhere in that blizzard, unless they stayed anchored to the ice. And even if they were anchored, the ice was moving. They would be swept along with it.

"Keep a look-out for *The Ice Queen,* but I don't think we'll see her. And just now, we'll go fishing."

They made their way across the ice to the edge of the sea, and dropped the lines down into the water. Captain Harken had saved some of the fish they had cooked for supper to use as bait.

They fished for hours. It was very cold, and their hands grew numb. But they caught seven big fish.

They saw no more bears, and they saw no sign of *The Ice Queen*. When they got back to the cave, Captain Harken said that it was time for them to leave the island.

"It's much colder," he said. "We should get as far south as we can, before the sea freezes."

While Nicholas was cooking two of the fish the men smashed the ice blocks, on which the boat was resting. They turned the boat right way up again. Some of the ice was still frozen to the sides. Tom Gold used the stove to melt it, and broke it off with the axe.

"Now you see why we turned the boat over, Nick," said Barnabas. "If we'd left her right way up, she'd not only be full of snow. She'd be frozen to the ice so hard that we'd never have broken her out. We would have had to chop a hole in the island!"

"I feel as if I might freeze to the ice myself, if I don't keep moving," said Nicholas.

"You'll be warm enough soon, when we start dragging the boat," said Tom Gold. "But you're right, Nick. It is getting colder."

"Let's have the hot food," said Captain Harken.

They sat down in the cave and ate the fish. Nicholas had made a hot drink, too, with a handful of berries.

As soon as they had finished, they loaded the boat with all their gear and food. Tom Gold tied ropes to it, so that each of them had a rope to haul. Then they started off across the ice, dragging the boat with them.

There were drifts of snow in places, but the wind had blown much of the ice clear. It was hard going, and Tom was right. Nicholas was soon warm.

He was glad when at last they reached the edge of the ice, and slid the boat into the water.

They climbed into it, and pulled out the oars.

"We'll give Nicholas a rest first," said Captain Harken. "You and I will take the oars for a bit, Barnabas, and then you can change with one of us, Tom. We'll give you a turn at the oars later, Nicholas, to keep you warm."

Captain Harken took one oar, and Barnabas took the other. They began to row steadily southwards.

There was no wind. The water was like glass. Nicholas saw each bit of ice, and each iceberg, reflected down into the sea, as if it were floating on a mirror.

The blue sky and the dark blue sea were very beautiful. So was the white ice. It sparkled in the sunlight, as if it had been dusted over with tiny diamonds.

They rowed on, taking turns, until the sun dropped below the hills to the west of them. The sky turned to gold. A rosy glow lay over the ice, and the snow turned red on the hills. The water changed to a red gold. Three birds flew across the sky, dark against the orange clouds. Nicholas thought that he had never seen anything as beautiful before.

"We'll sleep in the boat, in turns," said Captain Harken, quietly. "I think we'd better keep rowing. The sea is beginning to freeze."

Nicholas looked at the still water. A skin of ice was forming over it. It was still so thin, that they hardly noticed it, but he knew that the air was getting colder and colder.

He was very tired. He lay down, wrapped up in a blanket in the bottom of the boat, but he found it difficult to sleep.

No one rested for long. It was too cold. They were warmer when they were rowing.

They managed to heat some food on the little stove for supper. They melted some ice, and made another hot drink. Everyone felt better after that, but their fingers and toes were cold, whatever they did.

When Nicholas woke, after his second spell of rest, he found the boat making for the shore. Captain Harken and Tom Gold were rowing, and Barnabas was in the bows, breaking the ice ahead of them with his axe.

The sky had changed. There was a breeze from the north-west, and clouds were blowing across the hills.

"We think there may be another blizzard coming, Nicholas," said Captain Harken, as Nicholas sat up, and looked around him. "We don't want to be caught in it, out at sea.

We'll find shelter on land, until it's over. Pack up the blankets and the gear, so that we're all ready to go ashore.''

Nicholas packed up the things as best he could. They were rowing into the wind, and it was very cold.

They rowed the boat into a little cove. Barnabas broke the ice which was forming on the water, so that they were able to reach the shore.

They climbed out, and pulled the boat among some rocks high up on the beach, out of the reach of the sea.

They looked around them, but there was nowhere to shelter. There was nothing but bare rock. There were flat stones on the beach and cliffs beyond.

''We'll have to use the boat itself for shelter,'' said Captain Harken. ''We'll build a hut. We can use these flat stones for walls. We'll put the boat upside down on top of them, for a roof.''

They set to work with a will, and in a few hours, they had made a little hut. The boat rested upside down on walls of piled stones. Inside the hut, the sail made a carpet for the floor, with a blanket on top of it.

All the rest of the gear was piled inside, under the ends of the boat. Tom Gold had made a little cave in one of the walls for the food. Captain Harken put the stove down in the middle of the floor, to give them some warmth.

"At least the roof won't drip on us, this time!" said Barnabas Brandy, as they crept inside through a little opening they had left in one of the walls. "An ice cave is all very well, but the roof drips, if you try to warm it up."

They pulled a corner of the sail over the gap behind them.

"We're going to feel the wind," said Tom Gold.

While they had been working, the wind had been getting stronger and stronger, and now it whistled in through cracks between the stones.

"I don't think we shall feel it for long," said Captain Harken. "There's snow coming. The boat and the walls will soon be covered with snow."

"Do you think the storm will break up the ice on the sea, Captain?" asked Tom Gold. "Will it give us another chance to sail south?"

"I don't know, Tom," said Captain Harken. "It might. I hope so. The sea was clear to the south this time last year. But Ulf said that winter was coming early."

Barnabas moved the corner of the sail, and looked out of the little opening.

"Ulf was right," he said. "The snow is falling now."

He closed the opening again.

They made themselves as comfortable as they could. In some ways, the hut was better than the ice cave. There wasn't much room, but at least it was dry. They could lie down when they wanted to, and the stove kept them warm.

And so the time passed. At first they were very cheerful. They all thought that the storm would break up the ice on the sea. Then they would be able to sail south.

They slept, and woke, and ate, and slept again. But the days went by, and still the blizzard raged outside. The snow fell and the wind went on blowing.

As time went on, Nicholas knew that Captain Harken was beginning to worry. He did his best to speak cheerfully, but they all knew that the journey ahead would be dangerous.

Nicholas lost all count of time, but he knew that the days were passing.

The buccaneers spent the time talking about Ramir, and adventures they had had in the past. They planned what they would do, when they got back to *The Snow Goose.*

Their supply of food began to get low. Nicholas felt hungrier than ever, but he knew that the others must feel worse than he did. He was only a boy, and they were men, but Captain Harken divided the food at each meal into four lots. Then they drew stones out of a hat, to decide which lot each one should eat. The men gave Nicholas as much as they ate themselves.

The hut was soon buried deep in snow. A great drift covered it. When they went outside, they had to tunnel through the snow. They always kept close to the hut, and they came back quickly.

Captain Harken, Barnabas and Tom Gold tried to go out fishing once or twice, but each time they were driven back to the hut by the wind, without catching anything. They couldn't even chop a hole in the ice on the sea, to fish through. The rocks and the shore were covered with ice, and the wind blew so hard, that they could scarcely stand against it.

And then, at last, Nicholas woke after an uneasy sleep, to find that the wind had died away. He lay wrapped in his blanket, listening. There was silence outside.

Captain Harken stirred, and opened his eyes.

"The wind's dropped!" he said, sitting up. "Tom! Barnabas! The wind's dropped. We'd better get out, and see how things are."

He struggled out of his blanket, and shook Tom and Barnabas awake.

"Get a hot drink for us, Nicholas," he said. "We'll take a look outside."

Nicholas melted some ice on the stove, and dropped a small handful of berries into it. They had very few berries left.

The others went out through the little opening, and tunnelled their way through the snow.

They were back before very long.

"Are we going?" asked Nicholas, as they

sat down. He poured the hot drink into their drinking horns, which they held out to him.

"Not yet, Nick," said Captain Harken. "The wind has driven the ice in to the shore. There's nothing but ice, as far as you can see.

"We're not strong enough to drag the boat over it yet. We need more food, before we try to go on. We'll take the fishing lines out today. We can cut a hole in the ice, and fish through it, now that the blizzard is over.

"We'll see how we get on. We may have to leave the boat, and go south over the land. Or we may have to stay here, till the ice breaks up in the spring. We could do that, if we have to. We can live on fish, and the stove will keep us warm. The snow people said that stove would last for years."

As soon as they had had their hot drink, they went out with the axe and the fishing lines.

Everything looked very beautiful, but it was very bleak. Nicholas couldn't help wondering if they could stay alive there, until the spring.

They were fishing for hours, but only caught three fish. They had two of them for supper, and saved the third for breakfast.

Everyone felt a little more hopeful, as they wrapped themselves up in their blankets to sleep.

* * *

Nicholas had been asleep for some time, when he heard a strange noise.

He rolled over. The other three were still sleeping. They had been out on the ice much more than he had, and they were very tired.

The noise came again. It was a queer sound, a little like a growl and a little like a whine. Some animal was at the door!

"Bears!" thought Nicholas, starting up. "Captain Harken! Captain Harken!" he cried. "There's a bear at the door!"

Captain Harken and the others were awake in a moment. Captain Harken seized his pistol, and Barnabas grabbed the axe.

A long, low call, came from outside the hut.

"Kuluk! Kuluk! Have you found them? Hallo! Hallo there! Is there anyone inside?"

"It's Hornwollen!" cried Nicholas. "It's Hornwollen! Kuluk's his dog. It's Hornwollen and Kuluk and the People of the Snow!"

He tore the corner of the sail away from the opening, and scrambled through, into the tunnel through the snow.

The head and shoulders of a large dog filled the far end of the tunnel. When he saw Nicholas, the dog burst into deep, joyful barks, and shouldered his way into the tunnel towards him.

Someone pulled him back. Nicholas pushed his way through the tunnel, into the sunlight outside.

Three light sledges, made of silvery metal,

were standing on the ice-covered beach. Each sledge had a team of six dogs. There were two of the snow people by each sledge, dressed in the same silvery-white clothes that Nicholas wore.

But Nicholas scarcely had time to see them, before he was knocked over by Kuluk. The great dog jumped up in delight, and Nicholas fell backwards into the snow. Kuluk stood over him, licking his face in welcome, until Hornwollen ordered him back. Then he moved just far enough away for Nicholas to get up, and barked joyfully.

Nicholas struggled to his feet.

"I'm afraid you've had a rough welcome, Nicholas," said Hornwollen. "We're all as glad to see you as Kuluk is, but we'll treat you more gently! You must forgive Kuluk. It's just that he's so glad to find you alive. Are there others inside?"

But there was no need for Nicholas to answer. As Hornwollen spoke, Captain Harken crawled out of the tunnel, followed by Barnabas and Tom Gold.

"Captain Harken!" cried one of the snow people, stepping forward. "Captain Harken of *The Snow Goose*! We hadn't expected to see you so soon again, here in the north."

It was the Ecrun, the leader of the People of the Snow.

"We hadn't expected to be here, Ecrun," said Captain Harken.

Hornwollen stepped forward.

"I'm glad we found you," he said. "I come from Ramir. I am Hornwollen, the traveller."

"I've heard about you and your journeys all my life," said Captain Harken. "And young Nick told us how you saved him, last year."

"You *should* say, how young Nick saved *me*," said Hornwollen. "But whichever way it was, we were glad to see each other then. And I am glad to see you now."

"Not half as glad as we are, to see you!" said Barnabas Brandy.

"We must hear your story, Captain Harken," said the Ecrun. "But I think we must get into better shelter, before you tell it."

He turned to Nicholas.

"Hornwollen brought you to our rock castles last year," he said. "Have you told the buccaneers about them?"

Nicholas shook his head. "No," he said.

"The boy didn't even say that you had castles in the rocks," said Captain Harken. "He would say nothing at all about your homes. He risked his life, rather than tell Captain James anything about you."

The Ecrun smiled. "I'm glad," he said. "That makes everything easy for us. You are a long way from our rock castles, but you are close to our mountain home.

"May I have your word again, that you will tell no one else where it is, if we take you to it? Perhaps you can speak for them all, Captain Harken.''

''You have our word,'' said Captain Harken.

''Then we will take you there now,'' said the Ecrun. ''Is there anything in your hut that you need?''

''There's the stove,'' said Barnabas.

''The stove is the one you gave us,'' said Captain Harken. ''It has kept us alive. The roof of the hut is our boat. I don't know whether we can save that.''

''If that is all, we'll leave everything as it is,'' said the Ecrun. ''You won't be able to sail the boat out from here now, until the ice melts in the spring. We'll give you another stove. And this hut might save someone's life, if he were caught here in a storm. This is a dangerous place.''

''But we have to get back to *The Snow Goose*,'' said Tom Gold. ''We'll need the boat for that.''

''The boat is no good to you, now that the winter has come,'' said the Ecrun. ''You must go over land, if you want to get back to your ship.

''But we can talk about this later. Come with me, now.''

They went over to the sledges. Nicholas climbed on to one of them, with Hornwollen. Captain Harken went with the Ecrun, and the other snow people took Tom and Barnabas.

The Ecrun gave the order. The dogs leapt to their feet, and the sledges slid away.

Nicholas hadn't been able to see any way out of the cove, except by sea, but the snow people knew the rocks and cliffs as well as Nicholas knew the streets of the city where he lived in his own world.

The sledges went through a narrow gap between some rocks, and along the beach. They went out on the snow-covered sea ice, around the point and along the farther shore.

Nicholas was filled with excitement. The sun shone and the sledges skimmed over the snow.

Each sledge was pulled by six dogs. Kuluk was running free ahead. Hornwollen had let him find the way to where the buccaneers were sheltering. Now he left him free, to lead the way home.

Hornwollen's sledge followed Kuluk, and the others followed Hornwollen.

They came to a flat valley, deep in snow, where a frozen river came down into the sea. The crossed the river as easily as they ran over the land.

On the far side, a wide ledge ran up from the shore like a great road towards three rounded hills. As the dogs pulled the sledges up it, Nicholas saw that it was covered in tracks.

They came to a little cliff in one of the rounded hills. Hornwollen stopped, and the other sledges drew up beside them.

"We're here," said the Ecrun. "Welcome to the mountain home of the People of the Snow."

He lifted a small hollow rock. Nicholas saw a lever behind it. The Ecrun pulled the lever towards him, and a door opened in the rock side of the cliff.

Hornwollen and the People of the Snow drove the sledges in through the door. As the last sledge came in, one of the snow people pulled another lever. The rock door closed.

They were safely inside the mountain home of the People of the Snow.

Chapter 9
The fate of *The Ice Queen*

"So that is what happened!" said the Ecrun. They were sitting around a big table in a room inside the hill.

Silver lanterns hung from the rock roof over their heads, and a strip of silver-coloured metal along the wall gave off a comforting warmth.

The remains of a meal lay on the table. While they had been eating, Captain Harken had told the Ecrun what had happened on *The Ice Queen*, and how he and Nicholas had been left behind. He told him how Barnabas and Tom Gold had left the ship, and come to find them. And he told him about their adventures on the ice.

"So Captain James thought that you would lead him to me," said the Ecrun thoughtfully. "But you turned south? You didn't try to find the rock castles?"

"Perhaps I might have done, if I'd known anything about them," said Captain Harken. "But Nicholas didn't mention them." He smiled at Nicholas.

Nicholas turned red.

The Ecrun looked across at him.

"You could have told Captain Harken, when you were left on the ice," he said. His voice was friendly.

"Nick's obstinate," said Barnabas, grinning cheerfully. "He's the kind you can't shift with an ice axe — or an iceberg!''

"So I see," said the Ecrun. He turned to Captain Harken.

"And you," he said. His voice hardened a little. "What would you have done, if *The Ice Queen* had reached the berry-fields? Would you have taken our berries? We gave you all we had to spare last time. We needed every one of them this year. And you gave us your word that you would leave us in peace.''

Captain Harken looked at him. "I don't know what I would have done," he said quietly. "The Council of Ramir ordered me to come with Captain James. Perhaps I should have refused? The old Lord of Ramir would never have commanded me to sail here again, after what I had said to the Council.

"But the Lord of Ramir is dead, and his son is still a boy. A man called Soluken is Regent of Ramir. He ordered Captain James to return to the north, and he ordered me to go with him.

"I couldn't stop Captain James coming. He had seen the log of *The Snow Goose*. That told him the story of our journey. It gave directions for reaching this land.

"Captain James would have come, whatever I did. I came with him, hoping that perhaps I might stop him doing any harm, once he got here.''

There was silence for a moment. Then the Ecrun nodded.

"That is an honest answer," he said.

"Sometimes it is very difficult for a man to know what he should do. I still trust you, Captain Harken. If you come here again in *The Snow Goose,* you will be welcome.

"But take this warning back with you to Ramir. If any *other* ship comes here, with any *other* captain and crew, we shall leave that ship to be lost in the ice and the snow, as we have left *The Ice Queen.*"

"What!" cried Captain Harken, springing to his feet. "Is *The Ice Queen* lost?"

"Sit down," said the Ecrun quietly. "Sit down, and I will tell you."

Captain Harken sat down again slowly in his chair, and stared at the Ecrun. Barnabas and Tom Gold leant forward, with their eyes on the Ecrun's face. Nicholas felt his own body grow tense as he listened.

"When the wind came from the south-west, the fog lifted, and the first blizzard came," said the Ecrun. "*The Ice Queen* was driven towards the north-east. So was the ice.

"We do not know what happened in that first blizzard. But when the sky cleared, the birds brought us news. They told us about the four of you, on the island of ice. And they told us that *The Ice Queen* was crushed in the ice, and sinking. The men from *The Ice Queen* had escaped. They were on the ice, and making for the shore.

"And then the second blizzard came.

"There were not many of us, here in our mountain home. The snow people live in the rock castles. We only come here, when we are travelling south. We happened to be here, because we had been cutting out new rooms under the hill. Hornwollen was with us, and we had the sledges.

"As soon as the blizzard ended, we came to look for you. All our dogs come from the families of those Hornwollen brought with him, when he came to the north. Kuluk is the best of all our sledge dogs. He lives with Hornwollen, and he seems to understand everything Hornwollen says.

"So Kuluk and Hornwollen came with us, and we went along the shore. The wind had swung round to the east, and we hoped that it might have driven you ashore.

"Kuluk found you. The other men from Ramir, the ones in *The Ice Queen*, must be ashore somewhere near the southern berry-fields. You found the northern fields last year. There are others, farther south.

"But that won't help the buccaneers now. Any berries that are left will be deep beneath the snow. But the men had food on the ship. They managed to get away, for the birds saw them on the ice. It's possible that they are still alive, if they were wise enough to do what you did, and make themselves a shelter."

"We must go and look for them at once," said Captain Harken. "They haven't the warm ice clothes that we have. They have only the woollen clothes from Ramir. It will have been much worse for them."

"They haven't a stove, either," said Tom Gold. "That stove kept us alive."

The Ecrun looked from one to the other of them.

"Captain James abandoned you on the ice," he said.

"That's no reason for us to abandon him," said Captain Harken. "In any case, he didn't mean to abandon us for good. We know that now. He only left us behind, because he thought that we should lead him to you. And the men on *The Ice Queen* only did as Captain James told them."

The Ecrun sighed. "I thought you would say that," he said. "You needed at least one good meal, and a little rest. But I have arranged for the sledges to be ready.

"The sea has frozen all the way across, from the West Land to the East Land. It will be a long, hard journey. But we will go and see if we can find your Captain James.

"If we rescue him, will he go away and leave us in peace?"

"I think he will," said Captain Harken.

"Let us hope so," said the Ecrun. "Very well. We are all tired from our journey. You must be exhausted, too. We shall travel much more quickly after we have rested. We shall sleep now, and then we will set out across the ice.

"No, Captain Harken!" (Captain Harken had drawn in his breath to protest.) "No, we will not go at once, and you cannot go alone. We will rest first. We shall travel very quickly, when we set out.

"Those ice clothes you have may be better than the ones they have on *The Ice Queen,* but they are not as good as ours. When you have rested, we will give you ice clothes like those we wear."

He turned to one of the snow people, who was sitting at the table.

"Kell," he said, "take them to their beds. We'll meet again later."

He pushed back his chair, got up, and left the room.

"I wish we could start at once," said Captain Harken. "Every hour matters."

"It's no good worrying, Captain," said Tom Gold. "The Ecrun knows what he's talking about. It's true. We are tired. I feel just about finished at the moment. We'll all feel better after we have had some rest. We'll travel faster then. We can't go without the Ecrun and his friends. We'd be lost in no time."

"I know that," said Captain Harken.

"Come this way," said Kell quietly, getting up. "You must rest, and so must we. The Ecrun is right. You would only lose time in the end, if you set off now. You would be too exhausted to make the journey."

They all followed him across a passage to another room, where beds, covered in sheepskins, had been set out for them.

119

"Sleep as well as you can," said Kell.

"It's easy enough to say 'sleep'," said Barnabas Brandy, as Kell left them. "It's hard to sleep, when you know that there are buccaneers lost, out there on the ice."

"He's right, just the same," said Tom Gold. "I'm near to dropping, Barnabas, and so are you."

"Whatever we think, there's nothing we can do about it," said Captain Harken. "Only the snow people can find Captain James and the crew of *The Ice Queen*. We'll rest while we can."

They pulled off their ice clothes, and lay down on the beds under the sheepskins.

As he lay down, Nicholas felt himself go limp. He was sure, then, that he could not have stood up for another moment. He dropped into a deep sleep, like a stone falling down a well.

* * *

Nicholas dreamt that Kuluk had found him in the snow, and was pulling him along. He heard a voice calling 'Nick!' and struggled out of his sleep, to find Barnabas Brandy shaking his shoulder.

Barnabas and Tom Gold were already up, and dressed in the silvery-white ice clothes of the snow people. There was no sign of Captain Harken.

"Time to go, Nick," said Barnabas. "Come on, wake up!"

Nicholas struggled out of bed and stood up.

He felt giddy with sleep.

"Drink this, Nick," said Tom Gold, handing him a goblet full of a hot drink made from berries. "It will make you feel better."

Nicholas gulped it down, and pulled on his clothes.

"There's a hot meal waiting," said Barnabas. "Come on, Nick. The captain's there already. We want to start as soon as we can now."

Nicholas stumbled after them into the other room. In spite of the hot drink, he still felt as if he were only half awake.

There was food on the table, but only Kell was there.

"The others have finished. They are loading the sledges," Kell said.

"Fine," said Barnabas. "We won't be long."

Kell handed them bowls of hot meat stew. They shovelled it into their mouths as quickly as they could. Then they all went to the outer room, where the sledges and dogs were waiting.

Everything was ready. The sledges were packed with gear, and the dogs were in their harness. The Ecrun opened the outer door, and the dogs pulled the sledges out to the snow.

Nicholas's first feeling was that it was even more bitterly cold than before. The wind was blowing from the north-east. He was completely covered up, except for his eyes and nose, but almost at once his cheek bones and his forehead began to ache in the cold wind.

They set off, down the long slope that led to the sea ice.

This time, Nicholas travelled on the second sledge, with Captain Harken and the Ecrun. Hornwollen went first, with a smaller sledge, and four dogs. Kuluk was running free.

They made their way down the wide ledge to the shore, and out on to the ice.

It was very hard going. In some places, the dogs could pull the sledges over the ice and snow. But in others, great rafts of ice had been forced together by the wind and current. The edges had broken, and piled up into ridges. Sometimes it was possible to go round the ridges, and find an easier way, but at other times they had to cut steps in the ice, and help the dogs to haul the sledges over the top.

After two or three hours of travelling, Nicholas was already so tired that he found it hard to force himself to go on. He was thankful that the Ecrun had made them rest before they set out.

They struggled on, with the bitter wind cutting their faces. At last, just when Nicholas felt that he couldn't go on any longer, the Ecrun called a halt.

They sat down on the sledges with their backs to the wind, and Kell heated some food for them. It was followed by another hot drink, made with berries and melted ice.

When they started again, Nicholas felt better. They came to smoother ice, and he was able to ride for a time on the sledge. Then they came to more great ridges of broken ice and he had to help pull the sledge up over them again.

Before long, he was so tired that he stumbled as he moved. But he struggled on, saying nothing.

At last they came to a little rocky island, in the middle of the ice covered sea. There was a small cave on the island.

The sledges were pulled into the mouth of the cave. Sleeping bags were unpacked. They were made of the silvery cloth and lined with sheepskins.

The Ecrun ordered everyone to rest.

Nicholas crept into his sleeping bag, and fell asleep so quickly that Barnabas had to wake him, to give him some of the hot food which the Ecrun said they must eat. As soon as he had finished it, Nicholas fell asleep again.

When Tom Gold woke him six hours later, every bone in his body seemed to be aching. He was so stiff, that he could scarcely get out of his sleeping bag.

But when he had had another hot drink and some more food, he felt better. He went outside.

The sun was shining outside the cave. The sky was a clear blue, and there wasn't a cloud in sight.

It was even colder than before, but the wind had dropped, and that made the cold much easier to bear.

The snow people loaded the sledges again, and they set out for the far shore.

They could see the East Land ahead of them now. Over to the east, in front of them, Nicholas saw a high ridge. There were cliffs along the shore, but the land seemed flatter to the north, and he guessed that they were coming towards the southern berry-fields.

It was some hours before they reached the shore. They only knew that they had come to it, because of the cliffs. The beach, if there was a beach, was covered in ice and snow.

They rested again for a little while, and then turned north, along the line of the coast.

They had not gone far, when Barnabas Brandy, who was travelling in the sledge behind Nicholas, gave a shout. He pointed out over the sea ice.

Nicholas looked, and saw something shaped rather like a boat.

The sledges swung out towards it. It was half a kilometre from the land.

As they came nearer, they found other things on the ice. There was a chair, and a lamp, and then they saw a little wooden chest.

Tom Gold stopped beside it, and opened it. It was full of silver spoons and forks.

''Now what in all the seas made them bring

that from the ship?'' cried Barnabas. ''They needed food to eat — not forks to eat it with!''

''They seem to have left the forks behind them, anyway, Barnabas,'' said Captain Harken. ''Let's see if there's anything in the boat.''

They could tell from the marks on the ice, that the buccaneers had dragged the boat with them for a long way before they left it.

They looked inside it. There were silver goblets lying in the bottom of it, and sacks of gold. There was no sign of any food, or of any of the sailors.

Kuluk had been nosing about on the ice near the boat. Now he suddenly began to bark, and started off towards the shore.

''Follow the dog!'' cried Hornwollen. ''Kuluk will find them!''

They all got back on to the sledges, and turned them east towards the land. Kuluk ran ahead.

Nicholas saw a pistol, thrown away on the ice, and they stopped to pick it up. Then they found a cutlass, and a stool.

''It will not be long now,'' the Ecrun said grimly to Captain Harken. ''They are leaving everything behind. Why did they bring these things from the ship? They are useless.''

''Let's hope they brought food and warm clothes as well,'' said Captain Harken.

''They would not have had much time to save anything, when the ship was crushed in the ice,'' said the Ecrun. ''I hope they saved some of the right things.''

Captain Harken said nothing.

Kuluk had reached the shore. He ran up over the ice towards the cliffs. They saw that he was running towards the dark entrance to a cave. He reached it, and disappeared inside.

As they got to the shore, he came out again. He pointed his nose to the sky, and howled.

One by one, the sledges came to land and stopped below the cliffs.

''Wait here, Nicholas,'' said Captain Harken. ''Stay with the sledge.''

Nicholas sat down on a sledge. His knees were shaking. He was not trembling with cold, or even with exhaustion. He was trembling because he knew from Captain Harken's voice that there was very little chance of finding the buccaneers alive.

Captain Harken, Barnabas, Tom Gold and the Ecrun followed Hornwollen up to the cave. The others stayed with the sledges.

Nicholas saw Hornwollen put his hand on Kuluk's head. Kuluk stopped howling. Hornwollen waited with him, while the others went into the cave.

It was half an hour before they came out again. Nicholas watched them anxiously.

Captain Harken walked slowly down the beach. He was carrying a leather-covered

book in his hand. It was the log of *The Ice Queen.*

"We have found them," he said quietly. "They are all dead."

"They have been dead for some days," said the Ecrun, stopping beside him, and speaking so that everyone could hear him. "Even if we had come at once, we should have been too late to save them. There was no food in the cave. And their clothes were too thin to keep out the cold, in the Land of the Snow."

"They hadn't a chance, poor beggars," said Barnabas Brandy.

"We will go back to our mountain home now," said the Ecrun. "This is the time of year when the storms come. It's fine now, but no one can say how long the fine weather will last.

"We will come here again in the spring, Captain Harken. Then we will seal up the cave. It will be their tomb."

Captain Harken nodded. "Thank you," was all he said. The men turned the sledges back towards the west. They shouted to the dogs. Hornwollen swung his sledge into the lead, with Kuluk running ahead, and the others followed.

Nicholas sat on the sledge. His hands were trembling, and his knees felt like water. He could scarcely believe that *The Ice Queen* had gone, and that Captain James and all his men were dead.

No one said anything at all, as the sledges moved out over the sea ice, towards the far shore.

Chapter 10
South to the Arcons

They spent some hours resting on the little island, and then set out again, towards the mountain home of the snow people.

The weather stayed fine until they were within an hour's journey of the shore. Then the wind began to rise, and dark clouds blew up over the hills.

By the time the dogs pulled the sledges up the long slope to the hidden door in the rock cliff, snow was beginning to fall again.

Snow fell for three days, and then the weather cleared, and the Ecrun said that it was time to begin the journey south.

The buccaneers had spent the three days resting and talking to the People of the Snow. The Ecrun told them tales of the North Land, and the buccaneers told the snow people about Ramir, and the islands of the south.

Nicholas listened to it all. He had taken part himself in some of the buccaneers' adventures and he was more interested in the other tales. He wanted to learn everything he could about the strange world in which he found himself. He was almost sorry, when the Ecrun decided that the time had come for them to leave.

They started out on a fine morning with the sun shining down. They were so far north, that the sun was low in the sky, even at midday. The light on the snow was so bright that the snow people gave them a strip of white bone, to put over their eyes. The snow people had cut little slits in the bone, so that they could see through. That saved their eyes from the glare of the sun on the snow.

It was easier going than Nicholas had expected. Once they had climbed to the top of the hills, they found that the high land was almost flat. It was covered with a thick sheet of ice, with snow lying on it, and the sledges seemed almost to fly over it. Most of the time, they were able to ride on the sledges.

Even the dogs seemed to enjoy the journey. They pulled the sledges along at a great pace. They ate big suppers of frozen fish at night, and dug themselves holes in the snow, to sleep in.

The snow people set up their bowl shaped tents at night. Nicholas had seen the tents before. They were made of the same silvery-white cloth as their clothes. They were heated and lit by the strange metal stoves, which the snow people carried with them.

The snow people and the buccaneers travelled south for three days, high up on the hills. Then they moved slowly down once more towards the shore. All the way south, they could see that the sea was frozen over.

"I have never known it so cold, so early in the year," the Ecrun said, as they came to the edge of the sea, and stopped to rest and eat. "The water is frozen farther south than I have ever seen it before. It's no wonder that the ship was crushed in ice.''

''I hope *The Snow Goose* is safe,'' said Captain Harken, looking at the field of ice, which stretched into the far distance.

''There is a river, to the south of the Arcons' village, where the water never freezes,'' said the Ecrun. ''It won't freeze there — not even this year.''

''You know the country very well, Ecrun,'' said Tom Gold.

''Of course I do,'' said the Ecrun. ''It is all one land — the Land of the People of the Snow. The Arcons should never have landed here. We used to take our sheep south in the summer, to the place where the Arcons live. We went south to the river, too.''

''Will you drive the Arcons out?'' asked Captain Harken.

The Ecrun shook his head.

''The Ice King himself will drive them away,'' he said.

''Who is the Ice King?'' asked Barnabas.

''None of us have ever seen him,'' said the Ecrun. ''But there is a story, which our grandfathers told us — and their grandfathers told them.

''It is a story of an Ice King, who lives in the far north, and who sends the wind and the snow and the ice, to drive everyone away from his country.

''A traveller came here, long ago. The story tells how he saved one of the Ice King's daughters from a bear. So the Ice King let him live here in this land, and showed him how to mine the magic metal, which gives light and heat.

"The traveller married the Ice King's daughter, and their children were the first People of the Snow. They found the caves in the rock castles, when they were digging for the magic metal. They cut the rooms out of the rock. They were the ones who made our rock castles. They cut them out, working with their children and their children's children. People say that the Ice King himself helped them.

"We are the People of the Snow, and so we can live in this land. But if anyone else tries to stay here, the Ice King will drive him away. The Arcons will leave, or else they will die. I'm sure of that."

"I'm glad we're not trying to stay here," said Tom Gold under his breath.

"He might be right about the Arcons, too, Tom," muttered Barnabas Brandy. "The winter may be so bad, that the Arcons will have to go away."

"I hope they get away safely," said Tom Gold softly. "I can't help thinking about Captain James and his men, when I look at that ice."

No one said anything aloud.

* * *

They came in sight of the Arcons' houses a few hours later.

Nicholas was thankful to see the smoke from the Arcons' fires rising into the air. At least the Arcons were still alive.

The sledges stopped.

"We will say goodbye to you here," said the Ecrun.

"Come and meet the Arcons," said Captain Harken. "If you know them, you may be able to make friends with them."

"No," said the Ecrun. "It is better that we should not meet. If we meet, we shall quarrel. If we quarrel, we shall fight. I want no fighting. We will leave the Arcons to the Ice King."

Nicholas shivered.

Captain Harken said no more. He knew that it wouldn't be any use.

So the buccaneers said goodbye to the People of the Snow at the foot of the hills. They thanked them again and again for all they had done.

The Ecrun put their thanks on one side.

"No," he said. "You are our friends. In the far north, everyone must help each other, just to stay alive. We do not make friends with the Arcons, because they should not be here. They have taken our land.

"But you will be welcome, because you will only come back if you need our help. You will come back as our friends. But remember what we have asked you: leave us in peace.

Don't bring other ships from Ramir with you, when you come again. Remember the fate of *The Ice Queen*."

"We shall remember," said Captain Harken. "I shall not come here again, Ecrun, unless there is great illness in Ramir. Then I will come, to ask you for the scarlet berries of the snow."

"And we shall give them to you," said the Ecrun.

Hornwollen found it difficult to say goodbye to the buccaneers. He had been glad to see people from Ramir, and he found it hard to see them go. He knew that he might not see them again. But he didn't want to go with them. He had chosen to stay in the far north, with the People of the Snow.

The snow people left one of their sledges with the buccaneers. It was laden with sleeping bags, a tent and a small stove.

They took the other sledges, and all the dogs, with them, and turned to go back to the north. Nicholas patted Kuluk, and Kuluk pressed himself against him.

The buccaneers and Nicholas watched, as the sledges started back up into the hills. They stood there, looking north, until the sledges and the People of the Snow disappeared over the ridge.

* * *

"And now for *The Snow Goose*," said Captain Harken.

They picked up the dogs' harness, which was still fastened to the sledge. They put the harness over their own shoulders, and turned south towards the houses of the Arcons. The sledge was so light, that it was easy to pull it along behind them.

They soon came to the top of the Arcons' fence, sticking up out of the deep snow. The Arcons had dug out a path from the shore to the gate.

They were given a great welcome. Hoon was down on the shore with a small sledge, bringing home some fish, when he saw them coming. At first, he thought that they were the People of the Snow, and made the sign against magic. He shouted a warning, and began to run. Nicholas and Captain Harken called to him. He knew their voices, and stopped.

Ulf the Strong came running out of the gate, with a sword in his hand. Then he, too, recognised Captain Harken and Nicholas. He gave a great shout of welcome. Some of the other Arcons had followed Ulf, waving their swords. But as soon as Ulf shouted, they knew who the strangers were.

There was shouting and singing and cheering as the Arcons brought the buccaneers back to their houses. Pots were set on the fire, and a feast was made ready. But Nicholas noticed that there was less food this time. The

Arcons were being careful, even when they were feasting their friends. The winter had come early.

"We will drink our hot berry-drink to-night, Francis!" cried Ulf, as they sat around the fire. "Or would you like the red wine, which Captain James left behind?"

There was a shout of laughter from the Arcons.

"Captain James is dead, Ulf," said Captain Harken. "You must forgive him for sending you the drugged wine."

"Captain James dead!" exclaimed Ulf. "How did he die?"

Captain Harken told him.

"He was not the kind of man who could live, up here in the north," said Ulf. "In the north, men must help each other. It is foolish to make enemies with drugged wine."

"It's strange that you should say that," said Captain Harken. "That is just what the Ecrun, the leader of the snow people, says."

"Then he's a wise man," said Ulf. "But he doesn't make friends with us."

"Did you know that you were living on the snow people's land?" asked Captain Harken. "They used to have sheep here in the summer."

"I didn't know, but I was beginning to guess," said Ulf. "Well, the snow people can have their land again. We are going south in the spring."

"You're leaving here?" cried Barnabas in

surprise.

"Yes," said Ulf. "The winter is early. It will be very long. The ice has come so far south this year, that we have decided to go. We shall scarcely have enough food to last until the spring. We shall sail south, and find a kinder land."

"The Ecrun wasn't so far wrong, when he said that the Ice King would drive them out, was he?" Tom Gold muttered to Barnabas.

"You're right there," said Barnabas, under his breath.

"We'll leave you all the food we can spare from *The Snow Goose*," said Captain Harken. "*The Snow Goose* is safe? She hasn't gone back to Ramir, has she?"

"They've had a bit of trouble on *The Snow Goose*," said Ulf. "But they managed to clear it all up."

"What do you mean?" asked Captain Harken quickly. "What trouble?"

"Captain James left three men on *The Snow Goose*, didn't he?" asked Ulf.

"Yes," said Captain Harken. "He left Cazzek, Fryock and Garl."

"And Cazzek was supposed to be captain?"

"Yes."

"Well, he might think he was captain, but the buccaneers didn't agree with him," said Ulf. "It seems that Captain James left orders that the buccaneers were to attack us soon after you left."

"I knew nothing of that!" cried Captain Harken.

"I know you didn't, Francis," said Ulf. "Nor did your men. No one knew, except Cazzek. It seems that he ordered the buccaneers to attack us. The buccaneers refused. Downalong Joe sent Peran across to warn us.

"When they couldn't get the buccaneers to attack our homes, Cazzek decided to blow them up. He came across one night in the twilight, with Fryock and Garl. They didn't tell the others where they were going. I suppose they knew that no one else from *The Snow Goose* would come with them. They brought a keg of gunpowder over.

"We were all asleep.

"They must have been going to try to blow us up. But we'll never know just how they meant to do it. They made a mistake, and blew themselves up instead. They're dead — all three of them.

"I'm sorry for the men who sailed with Captain James. You've got to agree that they all tried to carry out his orders. But his orders led them all to their deaths. The only land they took from us was their graves."

There was a short silence.

"I'm sorry, Ulf," said Captain Harken at last. "I should never have brought Captain James and his men here."

"They would have come without you," said Ulf. "And then we should have had no one to warn us. We should have drunk the red wine. And where should we have been then?

"No, Francis. You shared fish and salt with us, and you have been our friend. You still are. I can't promise that other Arcons will be your friends, any more than you can make promises for other men from Ramir. This friendship is between the two of us — and the people here, and the crew of your ship.

"If ever we meet again, on sea or on land, the Arcons from *The Fire-bird* will be friends with the buccaneers from *The Snow Goose.* But that's all. It's between the two of us."

"Where is *The Snow Goose* now?" asked Captain Harken.

"Farther south, anchored in the mouth of the river," said Ulf. "The sea hasn't frozen there. We'll take you down to her tomorrow. We'll show you the way.

"Will you sail back to Ramir? Will you be welcome there now?"

"We shall sail back to Ramir," said Captain Harken. "I shall tell the Council of Ramir exactly what happened. A man called Soluken is Regent of Ramir. It was Soluken who gave Captain James his orders.

"Soluken will be angry. But Soluken is only the regent. He is not the king. Neither is he the Council of Ramir. The Alarkin will be king before long, and he will listen to us. So will the Council.

"Yes, Ulf. We shall sail back to Ramir."

"Good luck go with you," said Ulf. "You're a brave man, Francis."

"We'll need all the luck we can get," muttered Barnabas Brandy.

* * *

They talked for hours, until at last they settled down to sleep.

The buccaneers had brought their sleeping bags inside, and the gear which the snow people had given them. They set the little stove on the ground, and put the sleeping bags on a wide platform beside the fire.

There wasn't much room, because all the Arcons were sleeping in the houses too, but Ulf cleared part of one of the platforms for the buccaneers.

Nicholas had already taken off his parka, because the Arcons' house was so warm. He pulled off the white boots and trousers, and slid into the sleeping bag.

He lay there for a time, looking at the fire. It seemed a very long time ago, that he had been there in that hut before, with Captain James and the others. And yet it wasn't long at all. It was just that so much had happened. And now Captain James was dead.

But Captain Harken was there, and Tom Gold, and Barnabas. And it wouldn't be long, before they were back on *The Snow Goose*.

Nicholas gave a deep sigh, and snuggled down into his sleeping bag.

* * *

It must have been three or four hours later, that he woke up.

For a moment, he couldn't think where he was. Then he saw the sleeping buccaneers, and the Arcons lying on the platforms by the fire.

The whole inside of the Arcons' house was full of a silvery light. It seemed to come from the strange little stove, which the People of the Snow had given them.

Nicholas drew in his breath. He guessed what was going to happen. He wanted to stay with the buccaneers, but he knew that he had to go.

He scrambled out of his sleeping bag.

The light began to swirl around him. It grew brighter and brighter, and shaped itself into a ring. It was so bright, that Nicholas shut his eyes.

When he opened them again, the house, the buccaneers and the Arcons had all vanished. He was standing once more in his bedroom, in the house in his own world.